# BEGINNINGS

SYDNEY CAMPBELL

ISBN: 978-1-7774505-5-7

Cover design by abu-chan
Editing by Megan Records

Beginnings

2

For KLM and her backyard filled with muses.

Other books by Sydney Campbell:

**Allie Styles Romance Series**:
*Temptation (Book 1)*
*Deception (Book 2)*
*Reckonings (Book 3)*
*Beginnings (Book 4)*

**Courtyard Tales of Contemporary Romance**
*Reawakening*
*Redemption*
*Reckless*

# CHAPTER ONE

It was mid-October, and the weather was just starting to turn. Through the window, I could see the wind blowing through the leaves on the nearby trees. I was in the kitchen putting away the dishes from the drying rack when I heard Matt come home from work. Seconds later, he appeared behind me, kissing the back of my neck. Loki, my 70-lb black mutt, was trailing just behind him, tail wagging.

I turned to look at Matt, gorgeous as always. He was dressed in a grey cable-knit sweater and dark blue jeans. We had been back in Montreal for three weeks, our time in Israel having been extended due to unforeseen complications with Matt's client. The change in weather had been steep, but I was grateful we hadn't come home mid-winter. That would've been brutal. Still, I found I was affected by the chill, more so than other years.

"You weren't cold like that?" I asked.

"No, Mom. I was not," he laughed.

He grabbed our little box from the cabinet and sat down at the kitchen table to roll a joint, watching me as I worked. He was silent. I stopped what I was doing and turned to look at him.

"What's up? You just enjoy watching me bend and stretch while I put shit away?" I asked.

He smiled.

"No. I have a couple of things I want to talk to you about."

I walked over and sat down across from him. He lit the joint, took a quick toke, and passed it to me. I accepted it gratefully.

"What's up?" I asked.

"Well, first of all, I want to move."

I sat up, surprised. But when I thought about it, it wasn't a crazy idea. I did not live in the nicest area, and between the two of us, we could afford something nicer. Maybe even with a yard for Loki.

"That's not a crazy idea," I said.

It was his turn to look surprised.

"I didn't think that would be so easy."

I passed him the joint and got up to resume my work. I pulled the last of the dishes from the drainboard and reached to put them away in the cabinet above the counter.

"What else you got?" I asked, my back to him.

He didn't answer, so I closed the cabinet door and turned around. To my shock, he was before me, on one knee, holding out a simple yet exquisite single square-cut diamond set on a platinum band.

"I wanted to know if you'd marry me."

I stood there, paralyzed. I could hear every sound in the room. The buzzing from the overhead light, the faint strains of music coming from the apartment next door, the steady pant of Loki's breath as she lay on the floor beside us. I felt every hair on my body stand up like I was hyper-aware of everything, all my senses on alert. I stared at him, unable to comprehend this feeling.

"Just say yes," he said, smiling.

"Yes," I whispered.

He stood up and slipped the ring on my finger.

"YES!" I screamed and threw my arms around his neck, jumping up and wrapping my legs around him. He laughed and stumbled as he caught me, and we twirled around a few times before he sat me down on the kitchen counter. He slid his arms around my waist and kissed me, my body melting against his.

"I love you, Allie Styles."

"I love you, Matt Goldberg."

"Shall we celebrate?" he asked, with a glint in his eye.

"What did you have in mind?"

He gently lifted me off the counter, set me on the ground, and took me by the hand. Together we walked to the bedroom. He turned to me as we stood beside the bed and began to undo my buttons, slowly, one by one. I stood still, breathing heavily, watching his fingers work and imagining where they might end up. He slid my shirt off my shoulders and snaked his arms around my back to work the clasp on my bra. As he pulled it from my shoulders, down my arms, he leaned in and gently kissed each of my breasts. I sighed.

"Yes," he murmured. "More of that, please."

Matt loved the noises I made during sex, and I went nuts when he talked dirty to me. After a year of being together, we knew each other's turn-ons like we knew our own breath. We could read each other with a simple touch. If he looked at me across a crowded room, I was instantly making excuses for our departure.

I wound my fingers through his curls as he

undid the button on my jeans, then slid them over my hips. He knelt before me, tugging on my panties and closing his eyes momentarily as he pushed them down past my knees. I loved the effect I had on him. It made me feel like a goddess, and I was convinced that was at least 80% of the reason the sex was so hot between us.

I stepped out my jeans and panties and Matt stood up again, drawing me close and kissing me deeply. I was completely naked except for my ring. Matt pulled away and looked at me for a moment.

"I can't wait to watch you touch yourself with that on," he said.

I smiled wickedly and took his sweater by the hem, pulling it over his head. He complied, raising his arms and then tossing it to the side. I repeated the same action with his T-shirt, then ran my hands over his chest, pausing to play with his nipples, something that never failed to drive him crazy.

I ran both hands down towards his belt, working the buckle and then undoing his fly. I dropped to my knees as I pulled his jeans down to his ankles, lifting each foot to slide them off completely. I reached up to take him in my mouth, but he took hold of my hands and pulled me back up to face him. I gave him a questioning look. *Who turns down a blow job?*

"Do you remember the first time I made love to you?" he asked.

"Like it was yesterday."

He continued to hold my hands, preventing me from touching him. I leaned forward to kiss him and he pulled back. Then he leaned back in and whispered in my ear.

"How I touched every inch of you before I let you come?"

I closed my eyes. I momentarily lost my train of thought as he let go of my hand and trailed his fingers down my arm. I shook my head to clear it and took a step backwards.

"That was a one-time offer," I said.

"Was it now?"

He took another step towards me and I took another step back.

"Am I going to have to tie you up?" he asked mischievously.

"No."

He took another step towards me, and again I stepped back.

"You're no fun anymore," he lamented.

I stood up straight.

"I'm no fun?" I said. "Tell you what. If you can catch me, you can do anything you want to me."

As I turned and fled the bedroom, I heard

him rifling through the night table drawer. Loki barely lifted her head as I raced past the kitchen naked. Clearly, she was used to our antics by now. I hit the living room and took up position behind the couch.

Matt appeared moments later, walking calmly and carrying a length of rope. I smiled at him.

"You're smiling?" he asked.

I shrugged.

"You're fooling no one," he said. "Your nipples are hard."

I instinctively raised my hands to cover my breasts and regretted it, the contact sending waves of pleasure through my body. I dropped my hands and said nothing as he stepped towards me. As soon as he took a step to the right, I went left. He laughed softly.

"You think this is how it's going to play out?"

He shook his head and took two steps forward. He stepped up onto the couch and swung over the back, all in the blink of an eye. Before I knew it, he had me pressed up against the window, the leaded panes surely making an indentation on my back. He dropped the rope, took my face in his hands, and kissed me. I wrapped my arms around his neck and hopped up onto the window ledge, positioning my legs around his waist and resting my feet up against the back of the couch. It was perfect leverage, and I was shocked we'd never thought of it before.

I looked up into Matt's eyes and saw nothing but lust staring back at me. I squeezed my thighs together. He closed his eyes momentarily and I felt him grow hard against me. My head swam when I thought of the pleasure I brought him. I took his hand and brought it up to my breast. Once there, he knew exactly what to do. I lay my head back against the window as he took my nipple in his mouth, and before I knew it, I felt him slide into me.

I opened my eyes and took hold of his shoulders, bracing my feet against the couch as I prepared to meet him thrust for thrust. He took hold of my hips and looked me in the eye.

"You'll be mine," he said, his voice husky.

"I already am."

He put his head down and established a rhythm. I moved with him, moaning as he picked up speed, raising my ass off the window sill.

"Allie..."

"Fuck me, Matt. I want to watch you come."

He placed his palms against the window and I lowered myself back onto the sill, clinging to his neck for support. He rode me hard, bringing me unexpectedly close to my own orgasm. I pressed my breasts up against his chest and felt him shudder as he thrust into me one last time. I had been so close.

He pulled out and smiled at me, and I put my hands on his shoulders and pushed him downward.

"Two seconds," I said. "I promise."

He obligingly dropped to his knees and buried his head between my legs. His tongue did a lazy swirl around my clitoris before taking it in his mouth and sucking gently. It was all I needed. I exploded around him, holding onto his head for balance as my orgasm ripped through my body. He kissed me, then leaned back against the sofa and gazed softly into my eyes.

"Mrs. Goldberg," he said dreamily.

"Ms. Styles," I replied firmly.

# CHAPTER TWO

Later that night, I was lying in bed, holding my hand up and admiring my ring. Matt grinned like an idiot.

"You like it?" he asked.

"I adore it. It's perfect."

I leaned over and kissed his chest before settling back against my pillow. I looked out the window at the dark night, the leaves being blown off the trees by the wind. Fall in Montreal was my favourite season, but it was always too short.

"Are you mad about the proposal?"

I turned to him, puzzled.

"Mad? Why?"

"Well, the kitchen floor might not have been

on your top five list of dream proposals."

I laughed.

"Matt, I don't care where you proposed."

"I just figured if I planned something elaborate, it would just get ruined, and this way..."

I rolled over towards him and put my face directly over his.

"Shh. You're talking too much."

Then I kissed him.

*

Matt and I spent the next morning calling our parents and his sister to share the good news. All parties were ecstatic and peppered us with questions about where and when. We hadn't even discussed those details yet but I was secretly excited to start planning. I just hoped that we were on the same page—small wedding, minimal number of guests.

When the calls were done, I turned to Matt and suggested making dinner plans with Lynn and Dave so we could break the news to them in person. Matt made the arrangements and then took off for work. I tried to spend the day writing, but was constantly distracted by romantic thoughts of us on our honeymoon. By two o'clock, I decided to call it a day and spent the rest of the afternoon surfing the Internet for apartments, duplexes, and houses. I had no idea where Matt wanted to live, but I had my sights on the Notre Dame de Grace neighbourhood, a longtime favourite of mine.

By the time Matt got in, I was dressed and ready for dinner. He hung his coat on the hook and looked at me, the disappointment obvious in his eyes.

"What's the matter? You don't like the dress?" I asked.

"I love the dress. I just prefer it when I come home and you're naked."

I smiled and gave him a quick kiss.

"We have dinner plans."

"Right."

"Go get ready." I turned away from him to walk to the kitchen.

I grabbed a drink and sat down at the table, waiting for Matt to change. The ring clinked against the glass as I raised it to my mouth and I smiled. That was a sound I could get used to.

*

By the time Matt got changed and we were on the road, we were already ten minutes behind. We hadn't even hit downtown traffic yet. I was just relieved I didn't have to face the wrath of

Lynn alone. She was a stickler for punctuality.

We arrived at the restaurant a decidedly unfashionable twenty minutes late. I was so stressed I forgot to hide the ring. The maitre d' led us to the table and I could see Lynn's irate expression from a distance. I grabbed hold of Matt's hand. He looked over at me, puzzled. But before I had time to explain, Lynn screamed.

"OH MY GOD, THEY'RE GETTING MARRIED!"

Dave looked around, confused, then his eyes landed on us and I sheepishly held up my hand. He burst into a grin and jumped up from the table. Within seconds, we were all hugging and laughing and kissing while amused diners looked on.

"Oh, Allie, I'm so happy for you both!" Lynn gushed.

She grabbed my hand and studied the ring, grinning from ear to ear.

"It's so you," she said.

We spent the rest of the meal going over the proposal—Lynn wasn't impressed—and tossing around wedding possibilities. It was a much more pleasant exercise when done with friends than family. Matt assured me he'd happily drive home, so I cut loose and indulged in multiple toasts with Lynn.

Yet no matter how much I drank, I couldn't help but notice we were definitely taking the wrong route home.

"Matt?" I asked. "Where are we going?"

"It's a surprise," he said, keeping his eyes on the road.

"You know how I feel about surprises."

He didn't say anything, but reached over and turned up the radio. It was Bruce Springsteen, and there were ghosts in the eyes of all the boys she sent away, so I didn't argue. I sang along instead. Matt winced, but only slightly. He was a good man.

He drove into NDG, down some obscure street I'd never noticed before, tucked away in some other dimension. He pulled up outside of a ten-house courtyard—five semi-detached units—and parked. I looked over at him.

"What's going on?" I asked.

Finally, he turned to look at me.

"I saw this place online. I came to see it with an agent today. She left me the key. It's empty. The guy who owns it is in a retirement home. No pressure. Just come see."

I unbuckled my seat belt and got out of the car. Matt joined me at the foot of the walk and together we walked through the courtyard, to the end unit facing the street. Being the corner unit, it had a large side yard, about one and a half times the size of the house. It was clearly visible through a chain-link fence.

"Does that yard belong to the house?" I asked.

"Yup," Matt said. "Perfect for Loki."

I smiled and we went up the front steps. Matt worked the key in the lock and opened the door into a tiny vestibule. He walked into the hallway and let me in. It was small. Cozy. There was a living room, dining room, and kitchen. It was fully carpeted but devoid of any furniture. It seemed to have been empty for a while.

Matt took my hand and walked me straight ahead into the kitchen.

"Imagine if we knocked down this wall," he said, pointing to the wall that separated the kitchen from the dining room. "If we get rid of the French doors between the living and dining rooms, it'll be like an open-concept."

He dragged me into the dining room.

"And that wall? On the other side of that wall is the yard. Imagine knocking it out and putting in patio doors and a deck? How amazing would that be?"

"So it's a fixer-upper?" I asked.

"Absolutely," he said.

"You can...fix up?" I asked, skeptical.

"I can do some things, yes. And I can afford

to pay for the things I can't do."

I looked at him.

"Allie. The mortgage on this place is less than what we'd pay in rent if we move into a duplex. It's a steal."

I just kept looking at him.

"Come, look upstairs."

Once again, he took me by the hand and led me up the stairs. There we found a small hallway with a bathroom on one end and a tiny bedroom on the other. In between were two more bedrooms. Matt pointed to the tiny room.

"I thought you could write in there. It looks out into the courtyard. It's pretty."

He pulled me into the adjacent bedroom.

"I don't know what we'd use this one for. A den? A guest room? Doesn't matter."

He pulled me out and brought me into the back bedroom, next to the bathroom.

"This would be ours," he said, pulling me in close. "We have room for a king-size bed if we want. We could break out the wall for more closet space. We could make it work."

I let him kiss me as I contemplated how I'd respond. It was insane. It was the first place he saw. Granted, it was kind of perfect, but I wasn't great at the whole home reno thing. I did like the part about paying someone else to do it, though. But still, it was the first place he saw. We should definitely shop around.

Before I realized what was going on, Matt's kiss had turned into something very different. There were hands everywhere as he peeled off my jacket and worked the buttons on my shirt. My first instinct was to push him away—the whole place smelled musty and old—but the stirring in my pants made me think twice. His hand had already reached my breast and his thumb was gently stroking my nipple. I moaned softly.

He pulled away from the kiss and whispered in my ear.

"Lie down."

"Oh, Matt, it's so gross."

"Shh…"

He took off his jacket and lay both his and mine on the floor, creating enough of a barrier for me to feel comfortable. Had he taken a moment to suck my nipple, I'd have fucked him in a pile of horse shit, but he hadn't, so there we were.

He took my head in his hands and kissed me again. I closed my eyes and let myself get carried away. Just as things were getting really good, Matt pulled away again.

"What?" I asked, annoyed.

"You're drunk."

"I was drunk. I'm fine."

He looked at me, eyebrows furrowed.

"Listen," I said. "We're together, you and I. We're getting married. We're here, in this house that you want to buy. You've got to stop questioning these things. If I want to revoke consent, I will. But I'm giving you blanket consent here. I am yours. So long as you care for me, and never abuse me, I am yours."

He gathered me up in his arms and gazed into my eyes.

"Care for you? I revere you, Allie. I fucking worship you. I would never do anything to hurt you."

He leaned over and kissed me again, this time with a new urgency, and I responded in kind. I put my arms around his neck, pulling him closer towards me and pressing my chest up against him. Again his hands were on me, working their way to my back to unclasp my bra. I reached down and undid his pants, tugging at them half-heartedly until he laughed and pulled away from me to undress.

"Already lazy, are you?" he smirked.

I unzipped my own pants and pulled them down.

"We'll see who's lazy," I said.

He pulled off his shirt and I let my bra fall to the ground. We both lay back down on the floor, and he rolled me onto my back. Rather than climbing on top of me, he shuffled over beside me, running his hand up and down my stomach and chest, careful to avoid all the good bits.

"You want this house?" I said.

"I do. But only if you do, too," he added.

I put one hand on my breast and spread my legs.

"Show me how much you want it," I said.

A smile spread across his face and he took my wrists in each hand, putting them over my head as climbed on top of me. He lowered himself so that his bottom half was pressed up against me, his upper body supported by his elbows on the floor. He leaned in and kissed me, then moved his hips, pressing himself into me, but not penetrating. It felt heavenly. I sighed.

He pulled away and moved downward, pausing to take each breast in his mouth in turn. I buried my hands in his hair, holding him close as his tongue worked its magic. It was sensory overload, every single neuron firing as he gently bit and sucked my nipples. I thought I'd go insane and I couldn't help but writhe beneath him.

He looked up at me and smiled wickedly.

"You are a horny little thing, aren't you?" he asked.

I let a small cry escape.

"But you like when I tease you." He trailed his hand down my belly.

I squirmed, trying to angle myself. He just laughed. I moaned again. His hand stopped right above my pubic bone and I was practically mad with desire. I put both hands on his shoulders and practically pushed his head down between my legs.

"So impatient," he murmured, easily resisting me.

He reached for his jeans and pulled out his belt, giving me an evil look. My eyebrows flew up as he took the belt in one hand, and my wrists in the other. He quickly slipped the belt around my wrists and adjusted it to fit snuggly. Lack of buckle holes was no obstacle for Matt —he'd quickly taken a liking to bondage and had all kinds of tricks up his sleeve. He secured the other end of the belt to the pipe on the radiator against the wall and surveyed his work, content.

"That'll do," he murmured.

I pulled once against the radiator to see how much give I had. Not much. I grew warm, imagining the possibilities of what lay ahead. Once again he trailed his finger down my belly and between my legs, this time sliding a finger inside. He smiled when he felt how wet I was, and slipped another finger in. He leaned over and kissed me. I moaned against him. Every sensation increased a thousand-fold when he tied me up.

"I do want the house," he said. "But I want you more."

He kissed my neck, my shoulder, and trailed his tongue lazily down across my breast.

"Oh, god, Matt."

He continued his trail, down to my belly, stopping to swirl his tongue around my navel. I raised my hips off the floor, begging him to hurry. I felt his lips curl up in a smile against my skin. He loved driving me crazy. He loved it when he could get me so worked up I came within ten strokes. He'd done his job.

"Just imagine all the ways I could fuck you in this house. All the places I could tie you up."

"Oh, god…"

He leaned over to take my nipple in his mouth. I wrapped my legs around his waist and he pulled away.

"Do I have to tie up your ankles, too?"

I shook my head furiously. He put a palm on the inside of each thigh and gently spread my legs apart. I brought up my knees and lay my head back on the floor, closing my eyes. Within seconds I felt his tongue on me, unleashing a wave of pleasure that washed over my body.

"Oh, that's what I'm talking about..." I said.

He squeezed my thigh, warning me to be quiet. I bit my lip as he continued between my legs. In his late teens, Matt had dated a complete nymphomaniac who taught him everything he knew about female pleasure. My only regret was that he was no longer in touch with this woman because I would have loved to send her a bottle of wine and some flowers.

I locked my ankles around his back, raising my hips and pressing myself into his face. He responded, quickening the pace of his tongue, pausing to nip and suck and essentially drive me wild. I felt the orgasm build and cried out when I tugged at the belt to wrap my hands in his hair. I raised my hips again, completely out of control and without a tether as the shocks pulsated through me, causing me to call out his name over and over.

Satisfied, he raised his head and moved upward, always staying on top of me. I reached up to kiss him and he obliged me, his hands traveling up to free my wrists. I broke away.

"Leave it while you fuck me," I said, still insanely horny.

I felt him grow harder against my leg, though he'd been plenty hard already. He grunted deep in his throat, the way he did when I suggested something that really turned him on. He always untied me before taking me, and I'd just opened up a whole new world of possibility for him.

He planted his palms on the floor, on either side of my head, and lowered himself onto me. He reached down and guided himself in, so slowly I thought I'd scream. I wrapped one leg around him and pulled him towards me. Bracing himself against the floor, he began to move, thrusting himself repeatedly into me as I raised my hips to meet him blow for blow.

"Matt…"

"God, I love you, Allie."

I came a second time, erupting around him just as I felt him constrict against me, enjoying his own release. He raised himself slightly, taking my face in his hand as he leaned down to kiss me, first on the mouth, then on my chin and forehead. He then reached up to untie me. When he was done, I pulled him close and snuggled up against him.

"Let's take the house."

# CHAPTER THREE

It was a Sunday morning in early November. Lynn and I were sitting on my living room floor, surrounded by boxes and newspaper, packing up years of accumulated knick-knacks and memorabilia. Matt and Dave were in the kitchen, packing and arguing over sports.

"Why do you have so much *stuff*?" Lynn asked.

I laughed.

"You think you're any better? Wait until you two move in together and you realize how much crap you've got. Matt's just lucky most of his stuff is already in boxes."

"You mean still in boxes," Lynn corrected.

"Whatever."

I wrapped up the ceramic bowl I'd picked up in Mexico and placed it in the box. I glanced over at the bookshelf.

"Don't even," Lynn said. "Why don't you just donate them all?"

"Donate my books? Are you mad?"

Lynn just shook her head, confounded.

"You have a Kindle," she reasoned.

"If you don't want to help, you don't have to. But don't you dis my book collection. Where I go, it follows."

Just then, Matt came into the living room carrying an ashtray and a freshly-rolled joint. My hero.

"Lynn," he said. "Come on, you've known her a lot longer than I have. You think she'd ever part with that library?"

Lynn shrugged and stood up. She picked up a box and started building it as she walked over to the bookshelf. She grabbed the tape gun from the coffee table, taped up the box, and started packing the books. I looked over at her with gratitude and love.

"Oh, stop it. We expect many invitations to this house of yours," Lynn said.

"Of course!" I said. "It's a courtyard. Maybe when one of the other houses comes up for sale, you'll move in and we'll be neighbours."

Lynn smiled and kept packing. I took the

joint from Matt and lit it, pausing to enjoy it for a few moments before passing it back to him and continuing with my own packing. Lynn was not a pot smoker. She loved the smell and seemed to love being around people who were high, but rarely indulged herself.

Loki trotted in from the bedroom to check out the action. She had been staying pretty much out of sight, stressed by all the activity. She had no clue how good her life was about to get, with 24/7 access to a yard. She took a few sniffs, went to Matt for some love, then returned to the bedroom.

"Weird dog," Lynn said.

Matt and I smiled at each other and just for a moment, our eyes locked. Something inside me caught fire and I had to look away lest I resort to rudely asking Lynn to leave. Matt came over to me, passed me the joint, and leaned down to whisper in my ear.

"I felt it, too. It will always be there."

He kissed the top of my head and returned to Dave in the kitchen.

*

"I thought I told you I don't fix up," I said.

Matt and I were standing in the middle of the living room, which was entirely covered in drop cloths. We were both in sweats and old T-shirts, surrounded by open paint cans, trays, and rollers. I was not pleased.

"This isn't fixing up," Matt explained. "This is painting. I already did the plasterwork and stripped the moldings. This is nothing."

"Nothing for you," I murmured under my breath.

"Hey, you were willing to help Pete paint the old apartment. I don't rank as high as Pete?"

"I was going to break up with Pete, not paint the fucking apartment."

"I don't know. I seem to remember you falling off a ladder, covered in paint."

I put my roller in the tray, wiped my hands on my pants, and walked over to him. I got up on my tiptoes and kissed him lightly on the mouth.

"I fell right into your arms. And I never wanted you to let me go."

Matt put down his brush and gathered me up in his arms.

"I will never let you go."

He leaned in and kissed me, uncaging the butterflies in my belly. I smiled against him, wrapping my arms around his neck and settling into the kiss. Kissing Matt was my most favourite thing in the world to do, and I indulged every opportunity I could.

The doorbell rang, startling both of us. Matt pulled away, reluctantly.

"You expecting anyone?" he asked.

"No. I was expecting to get laid."

Matt laughed and extricated himself from my arms. He walked to the door and pulled it open. There were two men, seemingly in their late twenties, standing on the front porch. The taller one, with brown hair and matching eyes, had his arm casually slung over the shoulders of the slightly shorter one, who was blond with piercing blue eyes. He was holding a bottle of wine. I walked over to join Matt.

"Hey," said the taller one. He removed his arm from his partner's shoulder and reached out to shake Matt's hand. Matt obliged.

"I'm Jason. This is Rob. We're your neighbours in the attached house. We heard some noise over here and thought we'd come say hi."

Rob rolled his eyes.

"He thought he'd come over and snoop. See who the new neighbours were."

Jason elbowed Rob in the side, and both Matt and I grinned.

"Come on in," Matt said, opening the door wide.

I stepped aside, then put out my hand as

they entered.

"I'm Allie, and this is my fiancé, Matt."

We all shook hands and walked into the dining room—the only area with enough room to gather. There was no furniture, save a few fold-up chairs we'd brought for eating takeout. We were giving ourselves until the end of the month, and my lease, to finish the renovations before we moved in. I opened up the chairs and motioned for the guys to sit down.

"I'm sorry, we haven't moved any of our stuff in yet," I explained.

"No worries," Rob said, taking a seat. "When does that happen?"

"By the end of the month when our lease expires. We've got a lot to get done between now and then."

Both Rob and Jason looked around and nodded in agreement.

"Let us know if you need any help," Jason said. "I can certainly paint."

Rob suddenly remembered the wine and handed it to me. I accepted it gratefully.

"I wish I had glasses," I said.

"Next time," Rob replied.

We chatted with them for a few moments. Jason was also in technology and he and Matt hit it off right away. Rob worked in fashion, at a local design shop. We talked about our work for a while—I held onto my restaurant critic persona—until Jason looked at me point-blank.

"Have you met any of the other neighbours yet?"

"No," I said. "We tend to be here at night, after Matt finishes work."

"They're great, mostly." Rob offered. "Some interesting birds in this nest, but we're pretty lucky overall. Your neighbours to the left are fantastic. Expats from the UK. Around your age, I think. They've got a bunch of young kids, so they're like zombies, always exhausted. The Tates, the house after theirs, are wild. Open marriage and everything."

I glanced at Matt and he caught my eye, both of us thinking of Temple and the stories she could weave around that. I laughed.

"Okay, Rob. Let them move in at least before you start with the courtyard gossip. We don't want to scare them away."

"It would take a lot more than that," I said.

Jason looked at me appreciatively. Rob stood up.

"We'd best get going, and let you get back to your work. Though the offer stands. Call us anytime for help. Just not now. We already had a bottle of wine."

Matt laughed and stood to shake their hands again. I followed suit and we walked them to the door. As Matt shut the door behind them, he turned to me with a triumphant grin on his face.

"See?" he said. "I told you it would be great."

# CHAPTER FOUR

We managed to get the wall knocked out between the kitchen and dining room before moving in, as well as having the bathroom renovated and the kitchen appliances and cabinets replaced. We decided everything else would have to wait. It was a miracle we lined up everyone to work within the same four-week period.

It was a cold, windy day in early December when Matt and I stood outside the courtyard on the sidewalk, watching the movers unload our worldly possessions and carry them into the house. I looked over at Matt, who had a distant, dreamy look on his face, tinged with a hint of lust.

"You're thinking of fucking me right now, aren't you?" I asked.

"No. I'm not."

I reached over and felt his pants just as the movers exited the van. One raised his eye. Yet sure enough, Matt was hard. He grabbed my wrist and pulled my hand away.

"You have to stop doing that," he said.

"Why? You always slip your hands between my legs to check if I'm wet."

Matt shifted uncomfortably.

"Yes, but we're alone when I do that."

"Please. You get visual clues. You can see when my nipples get hard."

"Not when you wear those padded bras."

I rolled my eyes.

"Anyways," he continued. "It's not the same. It's humiliating."

"You love it," I teased.

"I do, but stop it. Please."

I sighed.

"Fine. Done."

I looked around and caught one of our new neighbours, Louisa, I think, watching us through the part in her curtains. I smiled and waved. She looked away. The head mover guy came over with his clipboard and presented it for us to sign. I took the pen from his hand and looked over the details.

"It's all in?" Matt asked.

"All in," he replied.

I signed the form while Matt paid the guy, adding a hefty tip. It had been pretty cold and we had a lot of books between us. The movers piled into the van and took off. Matt and I looked at each other and smiled like lunatics. He took my hand and we walked the long walk through the courtyard to our house at the back. As soon as we climbed the stairs, he slid an arm under my knees and swept me up, bride-like, and carried me over the threshold. I clung to his neck, enjoying the ride.

*

I sensed it was early before I even opened my eyes. I could feel Matt beside me and Loki was still quiet at our feet. I debated not opening them at all and just going back to sleep. It was the second week of December, I had a column due that afternoon, we still had a ton of boxes to unpack, and I was just so *tired*.

"I know you're up," Matt whispered.

I smiled, eyes still closed.

"How do you know?" I asked.

"Your breathing changes."

I opened my eyes and looked at him.

"You can be so creepy sometimes."

He leaned over and kissed me.

"Why are you fake sleeping?" he asked. "You don't want to make love to me on this beautiful Sunday morning?"

I purred.

"God, I love that sound," he said.

"I'm just so fucking tired, Matt. It's just too much. And we haven't even thought about the wedding yet."

Matt jumped out of bed so suddenly I felt the breeze blow past. He disappeared from the room and returned a moment later, carrying an envelope. He climbed back into bed, finally ready to face my questioning glare.

"I have a surprise," he said.

"Matthew Goldberg. You know I hate surprises."

"Every single surprise I have planned for you has worked out extraordinarily well, don't you think?"

I thought about it. The houseboat, the proposal, the house...he did have a good track record.

"What is it?" I asked.

"We're getting married."

"Yes, I know that," I said, rolling my eyes.

"No. I mean it. On December 31. In Mexico."

I looked at him, shocked.

"WHAT?"

He pulled a pamphlet out of the envelope. It was a glossy brochure for an all-inclusive resort in the Riviera Maya—beautiful, 5-star stuff.

"We're going to get married on the beach. It can be just us or you can invite whoever you want. But the point is, there's nothing for us to do. We just have to enjoy an incredible week, and one night, we show up at a set time, and get married."

I threw my arms around him and climbed on top of him, pushing him back down onto the bed. I covered his face in kisses, practically assaulting him until he cupped my head in his hands and stilled me. He kissed my mouth and I settled down, kissing him back with every ounce of love and gratitude I had.

"It's perfect, Matt. Just perfect. God, I love you."

*

Later that morning, Matt and I sat at the kitchen table, which was now in the dining room. We were still in our bathrobes, not even having bothered to get dressed on such a dreary morning. We were putting together a guest list for the wedding. It took us all of thirty seconds—my parents, his family, Dave and Lynn. Done.

"You sure you don't want a big thing?" he asked, worried.

"A little too late for that, isn't it?" I laughed.

"No, it's not. We can just call it a vacation and get married here later."

"No! This is great, Matt. I love it. I want a white sundress and strappy sandals and the ocean wind in my hair. It will be spectacular."

"Okay, then. How do you want to do this? What if it's too late? We're not giving them much notice."

"Oh, well. Then it'll just be us." I leaned over and gave him a quick kiss. "This is what we'll do. We'll draft a cute email, send it out, then turn off our phones for the rest of the day. What do you think?"

"I love it."

I opened my laptop and started composing the email while Matt rolled a joint. I smiled to myself. A little wake-and-bake on a frosty December morning in our cozy new house. And there I was, drafting a wedding invitation. I couldn't believe it. It was a total 'pinch me' moment.

"What are you thinking?" Matt asked.

"How amazing this all is. How lucky we are to have found each other."

Matt smiled and me and lit the joint. He

watched as I typed, and I felt myself blush under his gaze as my nipples hardened. From the corner of my eye, I saw his lip curl up, and I knew he noticed. I focused on the email, and when I was done, I turned the computer toward him and took the joint from his hand. He pulled the laptop closer and I propped my feet up on his lap, leaning back in my chair and watching while he read. He absently rubbed one foot.

"It's great. Perfect. Hit send and we'll shut off our phones."

I did as he said, and we both powered down. I couldn't even remember the last time I'd done that. The initial panic was immediately replaced by a rush of relief. I felt giddy. I took another toke off the joint and passed it back to Matt. He took it and cocked his head, considering me.

"Spread your legs," he said.

I dropped my feet to the ground and spread my legs, letting my robe fall to either side. He looked at me hungrily. He waved his finger in the air, motioning towards the neck of my robe, indicating I should loosen it. I did, pulling the collar down and exposing my breast almost to the nipple. He closed his eyes for a moment. When he opened them, he stood up and looked down at me.

"Don't move," he said and left the room.

Earlier that year, before he left for Israel, I gave Matt a parting gift. I let him take pictures of me naked, and it turned him on so much he now did it every chance he got. I heard him rummaging around in one of the boxes in the living room and smiled to myself. It was so easy to make him happy. I trailed my finger along my thigh as I waited for him to return.

Moments later, he walked back into the room with the camera and a puzzled expression on his face.

"What's wrong?" I asked.

"Nothing," he said, shaking his head as if trying to clear it of a troubling thought.

He aimed the camera at me. I brought my hand further up my thigh and heard him start to shoot. I raised my hand and slid it inside my robe, cupping my breast. I looked the camera straight in the lens, knowing that was his favourite pose. His second favourite was the shots that looked like I didn't even know he was there, like he caught me in the middle of doing something very naughty. I squirmed in my seat thinking about it and looked into his eyes.

"Okay. What's wrong?" I said.

I pulled my hand out of my robe and shut my legs. He was clearly not into this, even though I was giving him my best stuff. He put the camera down on the table. He sighed.

"Well, it's just that. Well," he looked at me, confused.

Then he abruptly left the room again. He came back seconds later carrying my magic wand. Over a foot long and bearing a head the size of an orange, it had become a legend as the world's greatest vibrator. But to the uninitiated, I could see how it looked like a very frightening power tool. I burst out laughing.

"What the hell is this?" he asked.

I stood up and walked over to him.

"That," I said, grabbing it from his hand, "is a woman's best friend."

I walked over to the sink and turned on the tap, washing the silicone head and being careful not the get the body or power cord wet. Yes, that's right. That baby had a power cord because it was far too powerful for any battery to sustain. I dried it and turned to him.

"Follow me," I said.

We walked into the living room, and I stepped over Loki's prone body to plug the wand into the outlet. I then walked over to the couch and got comfortable, turning on the vibrator. Loki jumped up and left the room, trotting up the stairs as fast as her legs would carry her.

"Holy shit, that thing is loud," Matt said.

"Yeah. It's why I never had any roommates. And Loki hates it." I laughed.

I touched the head lightly to my clitoris and grew serious rather quickly. I lay my head back against the pillows and watched Matt, as he marveled at the sheer size of the thing.

"What's so special about it?" he asked. "I mean, aside from its obvious power."

"It's the orgasm," I said, shifting slightly and arching my back. "Most orgasms creep. They build. Not this one. This one is just there, boom, like an explosion. Oh, god…"

I watched as Matt reached into his robe and took himself in hand. He walked towards me, stroking himself lightly and staring intently at me.

"Touch your tits," he said, now standing directly over me.

I did as asked, massaging my breast and running my thumb over my nipple. We both watched as it grew even harder, and I heard Matt's breath quicken.

"Don't come," I said. "I'm going to need you to fuck me."

With that, the orgasm swept over me, causing me to cry out as I closed my legs around the wand's head. I tried desperately to contain the sensation, to come a second time. Matt reached over and took the wand from my hand, shutting it off and dropping it on the table behind him. He climbed on top of me, taking one breast in his hand and leaning down to take my nipple in his mouth. I moaned and raised my hips, inviting him in. He reached down, slid his hands between my legs, and slipped one finger inside. I cried out, pleading with him to take me.

"Shhh," he whispered.

"Please," I begged.

"I love feeling how wet you are. It's such a fucking turn-on."

He pulled his finger out and guided himself inside. I clasped onto his back in relief, wrapping my legs around his waist and raising my hips off the couch. He chuckled against my neck, clearly amused by my impatience. I stilled myself, knowing if he realized how badly I wanted him, he'd only torture me further. Over a year we'd been together, and every day I wanted him more. We'd had sex in hundreds of different ways, and we were still only at the tip of the iceberg of what was possible. As he moved inside me now, my body responded in ways beyond my control. I dragged my fingernails down his back, and he slid both his hands underneath me, grasping my buttocks.

I raised my hips off the couch once again, and as he thrust into me, I felt his finger slide inside my ass. I stilled for a moment, shocked, and then slowly began to move again. I was surprised at how much I enjoyed the sensation. Ass play had never been in my repertoire, and I was beginning to have second thoughts. I had never felt so full, so… invaded. It was fucking hot.

"Oh, Matt," I moaned.

I dug my nails deeper into him and clasped my ankles tightly as the orgasm overcame me. It was all he needed, and within two more strokes, he came, grabbing my ass and biting my neck. He collapsed on top of me, and I wrapped my arms around him, snuggling deep into his neck and kissing his shoulder.

*

"Is it time?" Matt asked, climbing into bed later that evening.

"I guess," I sighed.

We both reached over to our bedside tables and turned on our phones. It took us at least ten minutes to go through the texts, emails, and voice messages. I laughed to myself over how many messages there were, considering we'd only invited seven people.

"So?" I asked when Matt finally put his phone down.

"Dave and Lynn are in, as I'm sure you know. My parents will come for the wedding — no more than 48 hours. Becky is undecided. You?"

I laughed.

"My parents said the same thing."

"Best of all worlds, isn't it?"

"It really is," I said.

"I'll send out another note in the morning, giving everyone the details. Let's just go to bed for now."

"I like that idea," I purred.

"You know that drives me insane."

I smiled.

"I know."

# CHAPTER FIVE

The next morning, I woke up with Matt and the alarm. It was rare for me to do that, as I had the luxury of being able to sleep in. But that morning I decided to get up, have breakfast with him, then continue unpacking. I also had to start packing for Mexico. Just the thought sent a small thrill up my spine.

Matt made scrambled eggs and toast, which far surpassed my usual bowl of cereal. I walked him to the door for a proper send-off, and as he put his hand on the knob, I pulled him back towards me for a kiss. He let go of the door, leaving it ajar, and wrapped his arms around me, stroking my hair with his hand. We lingered over the kiss, enjoying the feel of each other, and when he finally pulled away we were both shocked to see someone standing at the front door.

She was pretty and young—probably in her mid-twenties. She had blond hair pulled back at the nape of her neck. Here eyes were blue and possibly the hugest eyes I'd ever seen. She looked like a deer caught in the headlights. She was holding a plate with a simple chocolate cake on it. It looked delicious.

"Hi," I said.

She smiled shyly, casting her glance from me to Matt and away. She was clearly embarrassed at having caught us in the act.

"I'm Allie," I continued. "This is Matt."

I pointed to Matt, and he smiled politely before I pushed him out the door. He gave me one last peck on the cheek and took off down the walk. The stranger looked at me.

"I'm Lily," she said. "I live two doors down on the right."

Lily turned and pointed towards her house, which was indeed two doors down on the right.

"Come in, Lily," I said, stepping aside and taking the plate from her. "And thank you for the cake."

She smiled and followed me inside. She looked over her shoulder towards the front door.

"Is he leaving for somewhere?" she asked.

"Who? Matt? No, just for work. He'll be back tonight."

She was silent, so I turned back to look at her before entering the kitchen. She had a funny expression on her face I couldn't quite read.

"What is it?" I asked.

"Nothing, really. That was just some goodbye for the day."

I laughed.

"We've only been together a little over a year. It's still fresh."

Again the puzzled expression.

"Join me in the kitchen. We'll have some tea."

She followed me to the kitchen, weaving her way through boxes and standing by the counter while I poured the tea from the still-warm breakfast pot. I took the two mugs and carried them through to the dining room. She followed me in total silence. She was going to be a fun nut to crack.

I sat at the table and motioned to the other chair. She sat and brought her cup closer, nodding in thanks.

"It's just that Chris and I don't say goodbye like that every morning," she said, taking a sip of her tea.

"How long have you been together?"

"Since we were kids, really. Fourteen? Fifteen?"

"Wow!" I said. "Real childhood sweethearts."

She smiled shyly again, casting her eyes downward.

"I guess the novelty must wear off after a while," I conceded as I took a sip of my own tea.

I gazed at her thoughtfully.

"What do you do?" I asked her, reaching for conversation.

"Not much. I take care of things at home. Volunteer at the local seniors' residence. What about you?"

"I'm a writer, actually," I said. "A food critic."

"That's so interesting," she gushed. "I'd love to hear all about that."

"Oh, I'm sure you will. We live pretty close, you know."

Just then, Loki came trotting in and sniffed Lily, who looked positively delighted.

"A dog! I love dogs!" she leaned over to pet Loki enthusiastically.

I smiled to myself. Loved dogs? I knew she had to be all right.

*

Matt made us a delicious Mexican feast the night before we left for the Riviera Maya. He even whipped up a pitcher of excellent sangria, which I drank with wild abandon.

"Maybe take it easy? We've got to be up early," he said.

"Nah. I'll be fine. This is delicious."

I poured myself another glass and pushed back my chair, fully sated. It was late, past eleven. We'd decided to pack before eating dinner, knowing full well we'd both lose our motivation entirely. Our flight was at 8:00 a.m.

"Good?" Matt asked.

"Amazing. I snagged me a good one," I said, smiling.

Matt got up from the table, planted a kiss on the top of my head, and grabbed my plate. He brought our dishes to the sink and turned to me.

"Why don't you go get ready for bed? I'll clean up here."

I raised my eyebrows in surprise. He cooked, I should've cleaned. But I wasn't one to argue when it came to being relieved of domestic tasks, so I got up and left the room.

Matt's dinner had been a surprise, but I had planned a surprise of my own. I went upstairs, walked into the bedroom, and quietly closed the door. I reached under the bed and pulled out a couple of shopping bags. Out of one, I pulled a white baby-doll nightie, with lace trim around the neck. I peeled off my clothes and slipped it on. Then I reached into the other bag and pulled out a wig. The long red tresses fell in light curls. I fit it on my head and secured it in place with some pins.

I assessed the look in the mirror. I made some slight adjustments, found and applied a great lipstick, and did another check. Hot. I climbed onto the bed to wait.

A little while later, Matt walked into the room, took one look at me, and stopped dead in his tracks.

"Allie?" he said, a little unsure.

"No," I said. "Serina."

He raised his eyebrows.

"Serina? And what are you doing in my bed, Serina?"

I smiled my most seductive smile.

"Well, a little birdie told me you were leaving to get married tomorrow, and that this was the last chance you had to have sex with another woman."

A slow grin spread across Matt's face. I swung my legs over the side of the bed and stood up. I walked towards him as he started to undo his buttons. I put my hands on his, stopping him.

"And who exactly are you?" he asked.

"I can be anyone," I said, slowly unbuttoning his shirt. "I can be the innocent woman who's never experienced real pleasure. I can be a dirty slut. I can be the girl you always wanted in high school but never had the nerve to talk to."

I slid his shirt over his shoulders and pushed it off of him, watching it fall to the floor.

"If you want," I continued, whispering in his ear. "I can be all three."

"Oh, god," he said, as I trailed my finger down his chest.

I looked up at him with innocent eyes.

"What's it going to be?" I asked.

"Oh, god. The first one. Jesus Christ."

He took my face in his hands and leaned down. Ever so gently, he kissed me on the mouth. He then proceeded to cover my face in tiny little kisses, soft as butterflies. He stroked my hair as he worked, and I closed my eyes, enjoying the feel of him.

He pulled away and studied me. He tucked a lock of hair behind my ear, then slid the spaghetti straps of the baby doll off my shoulders. I sighed. He trailed his fingers from the base of my neck down into my cleavage, raising goosebumps as he went. Then he stopped and cupped one breast. I let a small moan escape.

"Does that feel good?" he asked.

I nodded up at him, keeping my eyes wide and round.

"Has anyone ever touched you there before?" he asked.

I shook my head. He smiled and took a step closer.

"So I suppose no one has ever touched you like this before, either?" he asked, as he slipped his hand under the fabric and onto my breast, grazing his thumb across my nipple.

"No," I breathed.

"Hmmm," he said, bringing my nipples to attention. "Why don't you take this off?"

I didn't move.

"What's wrong?" he asked.

"I forgot to wear panties."

Matt groaned and ran his hand over his face, mumbling under his breath about how much he loved me.

"I'm sure it'll be fine," he said. "Just take it off and lie down on the bed."

Hesitating, I took off the baby doll and dropped it to the floor. Matt swallowed and licked his lips as he watched me climb onto the bed, red hair cascading down my back. I felt so fucking hot I vowed to make roleplay a part of our repertoire. It was something I had never done before, and I wasn't even sure I'd go through with it until I hit that pitcher of sangria. Now I was practically panting.

I crawled to the head of the bed and lay down, leaning up against the pillows at the headboard. I looked up at Matt, awaiting further instruction.

"Have you ever touched yourself?" he asked.

I shook my head.

"I want you to touch your breast."

I brought my hand up to my breast and cupped it, using my thumb to stroke my nipple as he had. He watched me, breathing heavily, and then sat down on the bed beside me. He took my hand, then leaned over and gently took my nipple in his mouth. He was so tender it was almost at odds with the fireworks he was setting off inside my body. It was as if he was tasting me for the first time. I moaned and slid further down the bed.

"Does that feel nice?" Matt asked me, raising his head only slightly to look me in the eye.

"It feels so nice," I said.

"Does it make you wet?"

I looked at him, confused.

"What do you mean?"

He closed his eyes for a moment and

breathed heavily. When he opened them again, they were filled with pure lust.

"I want you to run your hand between your legs and tell me if you're wet."

"I'm not sure how…can you show me?"

Matt lay down beside me on the bed and took my hand in his, guiding it between my legs. I closed my eyes as he pressed my own hand against myself and taught me how to tease my clitoris. He then pulled his hand away and stood up to watch me.

"That's right, Serina. Does that feel good?"

I nodded, letting another moan escape my lips. He reached for the buckle on his belt and loosened it in a flash. Within seconds, he was easing down his pants, and I swear he was harder than I'd ever seen him before. I made a mental note to pack the wig. He took himself in hand.

"What are you doing?" I asked.

"Getting ready for you," he said.

"It's so hard," I said. "Can I touch it?"

"Have you ever touched one before?"

I shook my head again and looked up at him from beneath my lashes. I thought he would pass out. I kept my hand between my legs but used the other to reach out to him, gently touching the head of his penis, then taking him in hand.

"It's so soft," I said.

"I want you to taste it."

"Taste it?" I asked, shocked.

Matt moved closer to the head of the bed, still standing, and held his cock in his hand.

"Open your mouth," he said, his voice thick and husky.

I parted my lips and he guided himself inside. I took him in, swirling my tongue around the head while feeling similar swirling sensations in my belly. He moaned as I took him deep, running my tongue along the underside. He put his hands on my shoulders and gently pushed me back. I looked up at him.

"Am I doing it wrong?"

"No, Serina. You're doing it right. But I'm going to fuck you now."

I whimpered. He climbed on top of me, but before positioning himself, he stopped and kissed me between the legs. I cried out.

"What are you doing?"

"Change of plans," he muttered as he settled into work.

I clutched his hair, my hips writhing beneath him as his tongue slid over my most sensitive parts. I closed my eyes and got into the fantasy, imagining it really was my first time. I opened myself to every sensation, completely letting myself go. My breasts tingled and I felt my nipples harden. I raised my hands to play with them, the combined attention to both erogenous zones driving me over the edge. Within minutes, I felt the orgasm building.

"Something's happening," I cried. "Oh my god. What's happening?"

Matt redoubled his efforts, putting his hands underneath me and pulling me in closer, burying himself in me. I exploded around him, the shock waves pulsing through my body as I cried out his name over and over. He raised his head and smiled at me. He pulled himself up until he positioned over me, his face an inch from mine.

"Kiss me."

He leaned in and kissed me deeply. I wrapped my arms around his neck, breathing him in. I pressed myself against him and he slid his arms around me, crossing them behind my back. I felt him, like a steel rod against my leg. I wanted to reach down and guide him home, but Serina wouldn't have done that. Instead, I pressed my hips against him, letting my body tell him what it needed.

"You want me to fuck you, do you?" he asked.

I moaned.

"You're going to have to do better than that."

"Yes. I want you to fuck me."

He moved his hips, lightly passing his cock between my legs. I raised my hips again.

"Please," he said.

"Please. Please fuck me. Oh, god. Please."

He reached down and guided himself in. He smiled at me as I cried out.

"I want to hear you make all kinds of noises, Serina."

He started to move and I was happy to oblige him.

"Louder."

I cried out louder, grabbing his ass and holding him as he thrust into me. He reached back and took my arms, then my wrists, raising them above my head while never once breaking his rhythm. Using one hand, he held both my wrists together and supported his weight with his other arm. He thrust harder, adjusting his angle slightly until I moaned and raised my hips to meet him.

"That's right," he murmured against my ear. "Does that feel good?"

"So good…"

"Do you think you can come again, Serina?"

"Like before?" I asked.

"Yes, like before."

"Oh, yes," I whimpered.

He increased his speed and tightened his

grip on my wrists.

"Show me," he said, and then drove it home.

I screamed as I came for the second time, wrapping my legs around him and pressing my pelvis against his. I felt his buttocks tighten between my legs as his orgasm erupted, causing him to cry out and praise God in all kinds of colourful ways. Spent, we both lay tangled up in each other, breathing deeply, neither of us wanting to break contact.

Matt let go of my wrists and lifted his head to look at me.

"Serina?"

"Hmmm?"

"If I promise not to tell my wife, can we meet again?"

"Yes."

"Will you come to Mexico with me?"

"Absolutely."

# CHAPTER SIX

Two days later, Lynn, Dave, Matt, and I were lying by the pool looking at a spectacular view of the ocean. The resort was beautiful. Matt couldn't have chosen better. There was lush greenery everywhere, the beaches were glorious (though suffering from a slight seaweed problem), local wildlife roamed free on the grounds, and best of all, the food was fabulous.

Matt had booked us the bridal suite, which was absolutely stunning. All white stucco with a four-poster bed and billowy curtains that led out to a half-moon balcony. Our first night there, we'd made love on the balcony, watching the moon move across the ocean. It was mind-blowing, and certain to be one of my most popular columns ever.

Afterward, we lay on top of the sheets and watched a gecko on the wall emerge from behind a naif-style painting to snare bugs. We were fascinated, and it became like a sport. We spent hours trying to figure out how to bet on it. The fucking gecko never lost.

Lynn and Dave had arrived the following morning. They had a room in the complex right next to ours, which was crazy convenient. Each complex was two stories, housing either four rooms or two suites on each floor. They'd opted for a room, thinking they'd spend time in our suite. They were wrong.

A waiter came around the side of the pool and Matt flagged him down, ordering a round of margaritas on the rocks. It was only one o'clock in the afternoon, but time had no meaning in Mexico. It was always time for a drink. And guacamole. Every hour was guac o'clock in our books. Lynn turned to me.

"How's the unpacking going? You done yet?"

I burst out laughing.

"No. I am not done. We're about halfway through, I'd say. I plan to focus on it when we get back."

"I can help," Lynn said.

"You have work. But thanks for the offer."

"Weekends. I'll come by. I promise. And I'll drag Dave."

"You're a good friend."

Dave leaned over and squeezed Lynn's knee.

"I heard my name," he said.

"We were just wondering how many trips to the buffet you'd take tonight," Lynn said, teasing him.

"Oh, at least four," he deadpanned.

The drinks arrived and we all enjoyed the cold refreshment in silence. I was carefully watching a crew in the corner set up tables and a BBQ.

"Looks like we won't have to go to lunch," I said.

I pointed to the catering team and everyone turned to look. Dave broke into a face-splitting grin.

"Can we move here?" he asked.

"When are your parents getting here?" Lynn asked me.

"Tonight. With Matt's. They're flying together. They figured it would be a good chance to get to know each other."

Lynn burst out laughing.

"They do realize travel is one of the top stressors, right?"

I just shrugged. I was pretty confident they'd

get along. In any case, the wedding was taking place the next day and before we could blink, they'd be gone again. We then had a luxurious three-day honeymoon. I already felt like I'd been there a week. I had called Trish to check on Loki and the house, and she just laughed at me.

"You've only been gone 24 hours," she said.

In any case, she was certainly happy to have a house to hang out in. One that wasn't next door to her parents. Trish had taken over my apartment when I left to move in with Matt. It had seemed like a great idea to her at the time, despite my trying to point out otherwise. But after only a few weeks she was beginning to realize she should have aimed for a little more distance.

I slid down in my chaise, pulled the brim of my hat down low, and closed my eyes. I had time for a nap before lunch. They hadn't even fired up the BBQ yet.

*

I was right. Our parents got along swimmingly. Matt and I were sitting in the lobby, watching the parade of beautiful people walk by, when both our families rushed the check-in desk. I had to laugh. They were chatting and smiling and if they had managed that after five hours of travel, then they must have really liked each other.

I jumped up and went over to hug my mother. She whooped when she saw me and held me close. When she finally let go, my father was waiting for his turn.

"My baby is getting married," he said in awe.

"Look at it this way," I said. "You're finally getting the son you always wanted."

He swatted me on the side of the head and turned back to the clerk, who was ready to serve him. I turned to Matt's parents, greeting them both and saving a big hug for Becky. She had decided on the 48-hour trip and was clearly having second thoughts.

"This place is beautiful," she said.

"Isn't it?" I agreed.

"I can't believe my brother did this. Shit. I should've stayed longer."

I shrugged.

"Change your ticket."

Matt elbowed me in the side. I stifled a laugh.

"It's supposed to rain later in the week, anyway. Check the weather before you make any decisions." I said.

The truth was, at this time of year, every day

it called for rain. And sometimes it did rain. For five minutes. But those dark clouds on her iPhone might be enough to convince her to go home. Not that we didn't want to share, it was just that we didn't want to share.

"We waited for you to eat," I said. "Just drop your bags in your rooms, freshen up, and meet us back here. Lynn and Dave will join us."

*

The nine of us enjoyed a very pleasant dinner, Lynn and Dave serving as perfect buffers for the evening. Becky had already tried to extend her stay but was told there were no vacancies. Matt squeezed my knee under the table when he heard that. I, at least, tried to act with some grace. I mean, I liked Becky—she was great—but this was my honeymoon.

After dinner, the parental units returned to the rooms for some much-needed rest while the five of us walked down to the beach. Becky went for a walk along the shore while the rest of us sat in the sand, staring out over the moonlit ocean.

"Thank you for getting married here," Lynn said.

"Our pleasure," Matt replied.

He draped his arm over my shoulder and I

snuggled in close to him, resting my head on his shoulder. I watched Lynn and Dave for a while, snuggling a couple of feet away from us. He was looking a little sheepish, and she was looking a little upset, but they were still close and after a few moments of quiet conversation, she let out an easy laugh. I relaxed.

"Dinner was nice," I said.

"It was," he agreed.

Sitting there with him, it was easy to imagine that every moment would be as perfect. It was a clear night and even though there wasn't yet half a moon, it shone brilliantly in the sky. The ocean was peaceful, with gentle waves lapping up at the shore. I felt safe and loved in his arms and quietly excited for everything that lay in our future.

"By this time tomorrow, you'll be Mrs. Goldberg."

"By this time tomorrow, I'll be Ms. Styles, married to Mr. Goldberg."

Matt squeezed my shoulder and kissed the top of my head.

"I'd better get going," he whispered in my ear.

I turned to him, puzzled.

"What's the matter? You got a date?"

He looked at me, a mischievous gleam in his eye.

"As a matter of fact, I do. My last night as a single man, I've got to take advantage. I think I'm meeting her back at the room."

I raised my eyebrows.

"I'm going to go pick up some drinks at the bar first, give her time to get ready."

Matt removed his arm from my shoulder, got up, and walked away without saying another word. I swallowed and looked at Dave and Lynn, who had confused looks on their faces. I smiled faintly.

"I'm sorry," I said. "I've got to go."

# CHAPTER SEVEN

The next night, just before sunset, Matt and I stood on the beach in front of our small group of loved ones. The resort had set up a lovely chuppah for us, and Dave had gotten himself ordained before flying out. I was wearing a white sundress, covered in a smattering of tiny pale pink roses. Considering the way we met, pure white seemed a bit of a stretch. Matt wore linen pants and a white shirt—the prerequisite groom attire for a beach wedding. We were both barefoot and holding hands, gazing into each other's eyes.

"I'm assuming you wrote your own vows?" Dave asked.

Everyone laughed. I looked out at the small

crowd and smiled, then turned to Matt.

"Matt. I'm so happy I found you. Every morning when I wake up, the first thing I do is look over to make sure you're still there. That you're real. I never thought another human being could make me so happy. I want nothing more in this life than to spend every possible moment with you. To celebrate your wins and console you on the losses. To raise a family with you. To climb into bed each and every night knowing you're mine and I'm yours. This is the way it was meant to be. I have never been more certain of anything. I love you. Deeply, passionately, and with every ounce of my being. I want to spend the rest of my life taking care of you."

I could tell Matt was having a hard time keeping it together. He looked like he was going to melt at any moment, and I squeezed his hands tight to let him know it was okay. He cleared his throat.

"Everyone probably thought I was crazy to let her go first and have to follow the writer. But here's what you all failed to realize. I'm off the hook now. All I have to say is 'ditto.'"

Everyone laughed, even a few passersby who were strolling down the beach and had stopped to watch. Matt grew serious and looked deep into my eyes.

"Allie, I can't imagine my life now without you. You awoke something in me that I thought was gone forever. You think we've shared everything, but what you don't know is that I was so heartbroken over my last breakup that I never thought I could be serious about a woman again. And then you came along. You have completely changed the way I see the world. You opened me up as a human being. You let me love. And, Lord, do I love you. You inspire me, you amaze me, you make me laugh, and dammit, you're just so incredibly sexy."

I heard someone stifle a giggle while my father cleared his throat. Matt ignored it all. My insides had turned to mush and I was now depending on him to keep me grounded. Of course, he knew and gave my hands a squeeze.

"I am so excited to spend the rest of my life with you. To see what we can accomplish together. The family we can create and the life we can build. I will treasure every moment with you. I will take care of you and support you in whatever you do. I think we've already established that."

I cleared my throat.

"I love you, Allie," he continued. "Now and forever."

"Rings?" Dave asked.

Lynn stepped forward and handed us the rings. We each took one and placed it on the other's finger.

"I now pronounce you husband and wife. You may kiss your bride, dude."

Matt leaned down and kissed me, gathering me in around the waist and bringing me in close. The gentle breeze blew past us we shared our first kiss as a married couple. I twined my arms around his neck, ignored the hooting and hollering from the crowd on the beach, and deepened the kiss.

Eventually, Lynn cleared her throat. Matt and I pulled away from each other and looked over at her sheepishly.

"Did you bring your vows like I asked?" Lynn said.

Matt reached into his pants pocket and brought out the original versions of both our vows. He handed them to Lynn. From a chair on the side, she brought over a small wooden box. She put the vows in the box, along with a tiny bottle of wine she produced seemingly from thin air, and covered it all with the lid. She then reached back to her chair and picked up a hammer and a few nails and proceeded to hammer the lid on the box.

We all stared at her in complete confusion. When she finished, she surveyed her work with satisfaction and turned to us, handing over the box.

"When you have your first fight, break this open. Share the wine, and read each other your vows."

I burst into a smile and threw my arms around her for a hug. She was the best. Everyone got up and started whooping and hollering, including the crowd of about 50 strangers who'd gathered on the beach. It looked as if our small wedding party had significantly expanded. It was a good thing everyone's food was already covered.

Dinner was served a few feet away on a beautiful terrace decorated with flowing white linen and silks. Candles were everywhere and it was just breathtaking. The weather was warm and we were close enough to the ocean to taste the salt air. The resort staff was great about rounding up additional tables for our unexpected guests, each of whom came over to present us with some sort of gift, ranging from shells from the beach to desserts from the buffet to trinkets from the gift shop. It was all very sweet.

We toasted with a glass of truly awful bubbly, and after just half a glass, I switched to margaritas. From across the terrace, I saw a young girl of about five or six, deeply tanned with liquid brown eyes, staring at me. I walked over and knelt in front of her.

"Hi," I said. "I'm Allie. What's your name?"

"Anita," she said, shyly.

I nodded.

"Hello, Anita. Why are you staring at me?" I asked.

"I've never seen a bride before. You look like a princess."

I laughed and hugged her. Then I watched as she ran over to her mother and told her all about it. I smiled to myself, not even noticing Matt, who had come up behind me, wrapping his arms around my waist.

"Having fun?" he whispered in my ear.

"The best time ever," I said, turning my head to kiss him.

"Dance with me."

"There's no music."

"There is in my head."

He took my hand and led me away from the tables, then swept me into his arms and led me in a slow dance. I could hear the sighs and murmurs from our audience and smiled to myself as I closed my eyes, resting my head on Matt's shoulder and holding him tight. Mine.

I heard the music start up, then get increasingly louder as some kind staff member turned on a sound system somewhere. Slowly, people trickled out onto our makeshift dance floor to join us. I watched in wonder, all these strangers coming together to celebrate *us* coming together.

"This is just the most perfect wedding," I said. "The most perfect evening."

"I'm so glad," Matt murmured, nuzzling my neck.

We were both so wrapped up in each other we hadn't noticed the time until the music lowered and I heard my father start the countdown. I pulled away slightly from Matt and gazed into his eyes.

"This is going to be the best year of our lives," I said. "It's like 2020 is a new beginning for both of us."

Matt kissed me. He didn't have to say a word. I knew he felt the same way.

"Three, two, one… Happy New Year!"

Everyone was yelling and cheering, kissing and hugging. Matt and I stayed put, our arms tight around each other, gazing deeply into each other's eyes. Like the first time we met, it was as if everything around us just melted away. It was him and me. He bent down and kissed me, and I felt the thrill travel through my body, again just like the very first time. I shuddered slightly, and he drew me closer, probably thinking I was cold. I sighed and he chuckled, breaking the kiss.

"One-track mind," he muttered.

"Happy new year."

"Happy new year, baby."

"Want to get out of here?" I asked.

"More than anything in the world."

*

Matt stopped right in front of the door to our suite. He turned to me and smiled, putting his hand out to indicate I should stop as well. He swiped the card in the door and opened it, the swept me up off my feet and carried me over the threshold. I laughed with delight until we got into the room. Then I was awed into silence.

The entire room was candlelit, accentuating the flowing white curtains and overall romantic feel. The bed was covered in rose petals, several of them used to form a heart on the centre. There was some early Genesis playing quietly from the Bluetooth speaker on the dresser. I believe the lamb was about to lie down.

I gazed up at Matt, getting lost in those sea-green eyes which would forever be mine.

"You did this?" I asked.

He smiled. I licked my lips.

"How do you want to play this?" I asked.

"I don't," he said.

I cocked my head, not understanding.

"We don't play at all," he continued. "Earlier, I took a vow to spend the rest of my life worshiping you. I start tonight."

I stared at him, breathless. He put me down slowly and I turned to him. He took my face in his hands and gently kissed me. I responded in kind. He pulled back and looked me over, from head to toe, the way he used to when we first met. It was as if he was taking in every inch of me, committing my body to memory, determining what it needed.

He ran his fingertips lightly down my arm, raising goosebumps in their wake. Even though we'd had sex practically every single day for over a year, it all felt brand new. My senses came alive and my body was responding in all-new ways. The butterflies in my belly were slowly making their way down my legs. I almost giggled but didn't want to ruin the mood.

Matt reached behind me and pulled down the zipper of my dress. He pushed the straps off my shoulders, easing them down my arms and then sliding the dress down my body until it gathered in a puddle at my feet. He studied me, a lazy smile on his face. The heat between my legs was unsustainable at this point. But I was enjoying every moment of it. He reached forward, hooked his fingers on the waist of my panties, and slid them down until they lay abandoned, along with my dress. He sighed.

"I don't think I tell you often enough how beautiful you are," he said.

I may have swooned. He trailed his finger lightly from my throat down to my navel. I definitely whimpered.

"You're not so bad yourself," I said.

I reached up and lightly traced his scar. He folded me into his arms and pulled me close, my naked body up against the rough linen of his shirt. He ran his hands up and down my back, bringing them to rest right above my ass.

"I love the feel of you," he whispered right before kissing my neck. "The way your skin responds to my touch."

As he said it, my nipples hardened against him. He chuckled and resumed his course of light kisses down towards my shoulder. He leaned back, maintaining his hold on my waist, and planted a kiss below my throat. I sighed and let my body relax, relying on him to support my weight. He walked me over to the bed and I sat down on the edge. I reached for his pants, and he shook his head, gently guiding my hands away.

"No, Allie. Tonight is about you."

I slid up on the bed and lay down, resting against the headboard. I parted my legs slightly and Matt climbed onto the bed to join me. He lay down beside me and kissed me again. I had no complaints. Matt's kisses were like oxygen. I was no longer able to survive without them. I felt tears welling up in my eyes and pulled away, embarrassed.

He put his finger under my chin and directed my face back towards him. I looked at him sheepishly. He leaned over and kissed the tears off my face.

"What's wrong?" he asked.

"Not a damn thing."

"Why are you crying?"

"I have no idea."

Matt laughed and then buried his head in my belly, putting his hands on my waist while I ran my fingers through his hair. He peppered me with soft kisses while I let the emotion pass through me and returned to him wholeheartedly. Without any instruction from my brain, my hips began to move.

"And she's back," Matt murmured, now moving his trail of kisses significantly lower.

He stopped just short of his destination, and turned his head to the side, resting his cheek on my stomach as he contemplated my lower half.

"What are you doing?" I asked.

"Just taking in the landscape," he said.

He brought his hand between my legs. Ever so lightly, he started tracing the lines of my most sensitive parts.

"The peaks, the valleys. The way you curve and bend, fold and rise. It's fascinating."

I moaned, once again burying my hands in his hair.

"And then of course there's this little miracle here."

I cried out.

"Never ceases to amaze me. So much power contained in one tiny spot. And I barely have to do anything to get it going."

He leaned slightly and blew gently between my legs.

"Oh, god…" I moaned.

He laid his head onto my belly, pleased with his experiment. He resumed tracing the lines of my body, settling on his favourite spot once again.

"Or, I can rub it like this. Or maybe like this. I love the noises you make when I do this."

"Ungh…Fuck…"

"Yup. Those are the ones."

He lifted his head and turned to look at me.

"You understand how much I love you, don't you?"

I nodded.

"I do. I love you, too. More than anything."

Satisfied, he turned back and shifted his body, moving down the bed as he buried himself between my legs. I raised my hips and cried out as his tongue explored, seeking, finding, and settling into its work. The heat that had burned through my body all night turned to sheer pleasure that emanated to every extremity. I felt euphoric. I wrapped my legs around Matt's shoulders, holding onto his head as the orgasm washed over me.

He pulled me in close, refusing to give up and continuing to lick and gently suck. He was rewarded quickly when I quickly came a second time, crying out his name as new tears welled up in the corners of my eye. He worked his way back up my body, kissing his way along and pausing to take each nipple in his mouth. When he arrived back at my face, he was surprised to see fresh tears. He kissed them away once more.

"That good, huh?" he laughed nervously.

"That good," I assured him.

He leaned down and kissed me then rested on his elbows. I took the opportunity to undo the buttons on his shirt.

"I told you—" he started.

"That tonight is about me. And I want to

make love."

I pushed his shirt off his shoulders, and he sat up and slid off the bed to get undressed.

"The bride will not be denied," I said, licking my lips as I watched him disrobe.

He stepped out of his pants and climbed back onto the bed, moving fast towards me.

"No, she certainly won't."

# CHAPTER EIGHT

The remaining few days passed as if in a dream. We kept them long and lazy, then ate and drank late into the night with Dave and Lynn. They were having a great time, as evidenced by the deep tans and lingering smiles on their lips.

Dave scored some weed off one of the scuba instructors and we spent one glorious afternoon on kayaks, getting high in the middle of the ocean. Even Lynn partook. It was a perfect day, and I sat in my kayak, watching the sun glint off my ring and marveling at how this had all turned out. A year ago last summer this would have seemed impossible, and yet there we were, laughing, in love, and married.

I looked over and Matt and caught his eye. He'd been watching me. He grinned guilty and I smiled back with nothing but love. He paddled a little closer to me and blew me a kiss. I could've sworn I felt it land.

"Hey, lovebirds," Dave called.

We both turned towards him, and he pointed to the guy on the skidoo, waving us in. We'd exceeded our allotted time.

*

Before we knew it, we found ourselves at the airport, lining up at security for our flight home. Matt, a frequent traveler, had his Nexus card but wisely decided to stay and keep his wife company instead of whizzing through and waiting in the lounge with a drink.

The flight back was smooth. I sat with Lynn on the plane and we debriefed about our shared yet separate vacations. She alluded that something was a little off with Dave, but assured me it was nothing serious.

"He's just more complicated than he appears to be," she said. "There's nothing more to it than that."

The remark puzzled me, but I didn't push it. I was still basking in the glow of the wedding, and wedding night, and wasn't ready to break the spell. I figured we'd get to it eventually.

We landed and went through immigration, the four of us parting ways at the cab stand and promising to meet up for dinner soon. Matt and I climbed into our taxi, exhausted, and were immediately grateful he'd had the foresight to book the next day, a Monday, off. I reached across the bench seat and took his hand. We rode quietly for the rest of the drive home.

Loki's reaction when we walked in the front door convinced me she didn't care if we were gone a day, a week, or six months—it was all the same to her. She was only truly happy when we were home. We spent a good deal of time on the floor, playing and cuddling with her until she was assured we were back to stay. Trish had already gone but had left a prepared meal for us in the fridge.

"Think we can ask her to move in?" I asked.

Matt laughed.

"Like, sister-wife kind of deal? Can I watch you have sex?" he asked.

I stared at him.

"I'm kidding," he said, coming over and taking me in his arms. "You only get to have sex with me."

"Not fair," I murmured. "I know for a fact you're still seeing Serina."

Matt squeezed my ass and I felt him grow hard against me.

"I hope you packed that wig," he growled.

I smiled and pulled away.

"Let's make it an early night."

*

On Sunday morning, we stood in the living room, surrounded by boxes, frowning at each other.

"Why didn't we just stay in bed today?" I asked.

"That's what you'd do every day if you had your choice."

I shrugged.

"Nothing wrong it that. It's a valid life choice."

"Yeah. If you're clinically depressed. Come on, let's just start unpacking."

I reached down to cut open a box and the doorbell rang. I raced to get it, Matt giving an exasperated groan at my eagerness to escape. I opened the door and found Rob and Jason on the other side, holding a bottle of champagne.

"Congratulations!" they cried simultaneously.

They engulfed me a three-way hug and I laughed so loud Matt came over to see what was going on. Jason reached out and pulled him in and the four of us stood there like idiots, laughing and hugging.

"How long do I wait to tell you that marriage sucks?" Rob asked.

Jason elbowed him in the side, hard.

"Shut up, you ass," he said. Rob laughed.

Jason turned to me.

"What are you guys up to?" he asked.

"Just unpacking. You're welcome to stay and help," I said.

Unbelievably, Jason started peeling off his coat. I think Rob was surprised, too, because he just stood there, looking at his partner.

"Come on, Rob," Jason said. "Take off your coat. We can help them for a few hours. Besides, it smells like they've got some great weed."

Rob shrugged and pulled off his coat just as the doorbell rang again. It was Lily and her husband, Chris, also coming to offer congratulations. Before I knew it, our house was filled with several of our neighbours, many of whom we hadn't even met yet. Rob took great pride in introducing us around, making sure to offer some juicy tidbit about each person as he did so.

Sophia was the first one through the door. Tall, svelte, dark, and gorgeous. She was sex on legs. When Rob introduced us, she gave both Matt and me lingering hugs and kisses on the cheek. She was followed by her husband, Mark.

As they walked away, Rob leaned in and whispered, "Open marriage, remember? Be careful. Sophia is *hungry*."

Matt and I exchanged amused glances.

Then Casey came in. I didn't catch her last name. She was absolutely adorable. Bouncy, bubbly, and young. I'd have guessed around 26 or 27. From what I understood, she was living in the house two doors over, house-sitting for a couple who had moved to the States but hadn't yet decided what to do with the house here. So, they hired Casey to stay for a year while they figured it out. Seemed like a sweet gig.

"What's her deal?" I asked my trusty source.

"Casey? She's after that," Rob said, pointing at the door.

At just that moment, one of the most beautiful creatures I've ever seen walked through my front door. Tall, about Matt's height, but built like a machine. His shoulders were huge—like, a few notches up from my favourite Scot. As he peeled off his jacket, I saw his arms were covered in intricate black and white tattoos. He had a chunky silver ring on his thumb, which caught the light as he turned to hang his coat. His hair was long, curly, and dark, like his eyes. He was panty-dropping hot. And he looked completely out of place in an NDG courtyard.

"What the fuck?" I whispered.

"Allie, meet Zach," Rob said. "Zach, this is Allie. And Matt, of course."

I put out my hand and he took it in both of his. He smiled at me, looking deep in my eyes. I may have blushed. In the quietest voice, he said, "Pleased to meet you. Congrats on the wedding."

He turned to shake Matt's hand, then moved into the crowd, where Casey quickly started chatting with him.

"What the fuck?" I repeated.

Rob laughed.

"Yeah, I've jerked off to him a couple of times. Don't tell Jason."

"Who? What?" I was still incapable of forming a coherent thought.

"Zach is a music producer. Moved into the courtyard about a year ago. He's got a pretty spotty past. Had some addiction issues, lost his wife and kids in a custody battle. He's been clean and sober for close to two years now, and he's trying to fix up his life. He's honestly a really nice guy once you get past the gruff exterior."

Even though Matt was the only man for me, a fact I assured him of by taking his hand and squeezing hard, I could not take my eyes of Zach. He moved like an animal through the room, like a graceful tiger, ready to pounce but practicing crazy restraint. Casey was just bopping along after him. He didn't seem to mind, but he didn't engage, either.

I had to turn away when the next batch of neighbours came in—the British expats with all the kids who lived in the house on our left, attached to the Tates. Ellie and Jack Marshall seemed sweet—early thirties, recently married, and living abroad for the first time. The kids, while adorable, were clearly a handful. Rob introduced us all and when Ellie leaned over to hand me the bottle of wine she'd brought, she whispered, "Do you mind if I open it now?"

I laughed, gave her a quick hug, and told her that Jason had made a pitcher of margaritas in the kitchen.

"I'm going to like you." She grinned. "Jack! Watch the kids."

Then there were the Levinsons, the elderly brother and sister who were sharing a house. Apparently, they'd been there for sixty years. They were only the second owners of the place. He'd lost his wife, and she had never married. Finally, there was Hailey, early-thirties, single, and a total trip. I loved her instantly. She was the kind of woman who looked like she knew how to have fun.

When all the introductions were complete, I plopped down on the couch to relax. Matt went to help Jason out in the kitchen and lay out the food everyone had brought. Lily came over and sat down beside me.

"So," she asked. "How was the wedding?"

"It was amazing. I don't know how else to describe it. Magical? Something along those lines."

"Sounds wonderful," she said dreamily.

"Where did you get married?" I asked.

"In church. With about 300 guests."

"Wow."

"Yeah. More of a show than a wedding."

"I'm sorry to hear that," I said sincerely.

Lily just smiled.

"Did the wedding night make up for it?" I asked.

Lily blushed.

"It was okay."

"Okay?" I repeated. "A wedding night should be more than okay."

"Well, we were raised Catholic, and have been together since our teens. Our wedding night was the first time for both of us, and neither of us really knew what we were doing

—"

"Ah," I said. "Got it. Well, at least you've got a few years of practice under your belt now, right?"

Lily turned red again, this time a much deeper shade.

"Well—" she started.

I turned in my seat and looked at her.

"Well, what?" I asked. "Lily. Are you two having some kind of trouble?"

"No," she said. "Not trouble, per se. We just decided a while back it would be easier to just, well, stop trying. Neither of us was having much fun with it."

I buried my head in my hands. This poor woman. I collected myself and looked her straight in the eye.

"Have you ever showed him what you like?" I asked point-blank.

"What I like?"

"Yes. How you want to be touched."

"How should I know how I want to be touched? He should know that."

I stared at her, incredulous.

"If he'd never been with a woman before, how would he know that?" I asked her.

Lily thought for a moment, then looked over at Chris, chatting happily with Casey.

"I never really thought about it," she

admitted.

"Have you never masturbated, Lily?"

She shook her head, horrified at the question. I took a deep breath and then took both her hands in mine.

"Lily. I want you to go home tonight, and I want you to touch yourself."

"Where?"

"Everywhere. You can wait until Chris goes to sleep if you like, though it would be a lot more fun if you let him watch."

She looked at me, shocked.

"Okay. A step too far. Listen. You get into bed, and you touch every part of your body. Every part. Do you hear me?"

Lily nodded slowly.

"That includes your tits, Lily. And your vagina. Got it?"

She blushed crimson once again but nodded firmly.

"You report back to me tomorrow."

*

At the end of the day, Matt and I crawled into bed, exhausted. It was lovely meeting all the neighbours, and it was great to get a hand with a bit of the unpacking, but it had been a bit much after the trip. I snuggled up close and lay my head on his chest.

"I'm so glad we met when we did," I said.

"You don't rue all the lost years?" he asked.

"No. Not at all. I think we met at the perfect time."

We were silent for a while.

"I saw you chatting with the shy neighbour. What's she like?" Matt asked.

"Repressed." I laughed.

Matt chuckled.

"I'm sure you can help her with that."

I looked up at him, resting my chin on his chest bone. He was staring down at me, love in his gaze.

"Tell me about her," I said.

He sighed and stroked my hair.

"Why?" he asked.

"I'm curious. She was important enough to bring up in your vows. I think I get to know."

I sat up, and Matt shifted so he was leaning back against the headboard. He looked at me and shrugged.

"That's fair enough, I guess."

I settled in for a story.

"It's not that exciting," he said, reading my mind once again.

"Tell me."

He put his arm around me and pulled me close, then let his hand hang off my shoulder as he absently tickled my back.

"Well, her name was Sydney, and I met her in university. She was only my third or fourth girlfriend, but we got serious very fast. All my other relationships had been much more casual. She was not into casual. She had her whole future set out, and I was part of it. She talked about our life together so often that I began to buy into it. I fell in love, and could easily envision buying a house and raising kids with her."

"So what happened?" I asked, looking at him.

"She didn't necessarily want me. She wanted the dream. And a couple of years after she graduated, she found someone better suited to fulfill it for her. Faster."

"So she dumped you?"

"She did."

"How long were you together?" I asked.

"Four years."

"Holy shit."

I snuggled in closer and wrapped my arms around him. I planted small kisses along his neck and chest, trying to make up for years of lost love in just a few moments. How could anyone have left this man?

"I'm so sorry, Matt. She was a bitch. I hate thinking that because of her you spent a decade alone."

"Well, there was that. And the travel. It just didn't seem worth the investment, given all the odds against me."

He pulled away to look me in the eye.

"Then you came along. And all the rules changed," he said.

I melted.

"We saved each other," I whispered.

"That we did."

I reached up and kissed him. He returned the kiss in a somewhat half-hearted fashion. I increased my efforts.

"Aren't you tired?" he asked, pulling away.

I grinned at him.

"Lie down. I'll do all the work."

# CHAPTER NINE

It was towards late January and I was having afternoon tea and a joint with Jason at the dining room table. He had been helping me unpack, which had started to seem like an endless task. Our boxes were having babies while we slept. I was so unmotivated to continue that Jason had taken it upon himself to pop by almost every afternoon to help me.

"So you've gotten cozy with Lily, I notice," he ventured.

"She's sweet. A little repressed, but sweet."

"You're right on both counts," he said, musing.

"What happened with the Levinsons?" I asked.

The night after our impromptu party, a small fire had started in the elderly siblings' house. Mr. Levinson's daughter decided it was time for them to move, and I'd heard that the place had been snatched up quickly.

"They're settled in with his daughter. It's all good."

"And the house?" I prompted.

Jason smiled.

"You mistake me for Rob."

I stared.

"The fireman that was on call that night. Bought it before it even went on the market. Private deal with the daughter."

I nodded, smiling inwardly. *Fireman.* He'd been hot.

"Hailey must be enjoying that," I said.

Jason looked away.

"I hear they don't get along so great," he mumbled.

I decided to let that slide.

"And what's with the house on the corner? That's the only neighbour who didn't show up for the party."

"Louisa? She's a nice lady, just keeps to herself."

"You are tight-lipped. Maybe send Rob over to help me next time?" I said.

Jason laughed and took a toke off the joint

before handing it to me.

"Fine. She's in her forties and single. Had her heart broken ages ago and never moved on."

I paused to consider that, realizing it could've easily been Matt's fate, too. Just then, we heard Matt's key turn in the door. He mumbled to himself as he entered and shed his outerwear. I shot Jason a nervous look. Matt was never in a bad mood.

"Should I go?" Jason asked.

"Please don't," I said. He laughed.

Matt walked into the dining room and stopped when he saw us. He forced a smile and came over to kiss me on the head, laying a hand on Jason's shoulder while he was there.

"No use," I said. "Can't fool us. What's wrong?"

Matt dropped into the chair next to Jason and took the joint from his hand. He took a long drag and then exhaled slowly, passing it back to Jason.

"I have to go back to Israel."

"What?" I said.

"I know. Four week tops. You want to come with?"

"Of course I do, but I can't. Look how much still needs to get done here. I refuse to go into spring with boxes."

"So a month apart?" Matt said, eyeing me uncertainly.

"That's my cue," Jason said, getting up.

"You don't have to go," I said.

"No, I have to go."

Jason gathered his things and kissed me on the cheek. He gave Matt a quick hug and whispered something in his ear. Matt laughed and clapped him on the shoulder. Jason walked out of the dining room and we heard him close the front door behind him. I looked at Matt expectantly.

"He said, 'You better fuck her good because I can't help you out when you're gone.'"

I laughed.

"When do you leave?" I asked, hesitant.

"Tomorrow. It's urgent."

"Fuck."

"Yes, let's."

*

I sat on the edge of the bed, watching Matt pack. On the way upstairs to the bedroom, he swore he wouldn't extend the trip. That he'd be back before February 23, in time for my birthday. It seemed his client had missed a few key instructions during setup and he just had to go down and get everything running smoothly.

"If anyone else had built the system, I'd worry," Matt said, zipping up his bag. "But since I built it, I'm not so worried. I may even be home sooner."

"I hope so."

I stood up and walked over to him. He turned to me and ran his hands up and down my arms. I gave an exaggerated shiver. He laughed.

"I'm going to miss you," he said.

"I'm going to miss you, too."

"Write your column for me?" he asked.

"Absolutely."

"Write about our wedding night."

I looked at him, surprised.

"You don't think that's a little private?"

He shrugged.

"I don't mind. Besides, I'm dying to hear your telling of the events."

He grinned wickedly and my belly did a little flip. He reached out and lightly brushed one of my breasts through my T-shirt. I closed my eyes.

"And masturbate at least once a day," he whispered.

"Done," I laughed and opened my eyes.

"Think about me."

"I always do," I said.

He stopped playing with my nipple and looked at me.

"Do you?"

"I do. First time I've ever been in a relationship and fantasized about the guy I'm with," I said.

He smiled, pleased.

"What about the Scot?"

"Listen," I said. "I can't control my dreams. What about you? Do you always think about me?"

I reached for his belt buckle and worked quickly, loosening it and undoing his jeans. I slid them down over his hips and heard the clink as the belt hit the floor.

"Yes..." he said, with a slight note of hesitation.

I stilled my hands and looked at him.

"Spill it."

"Well," he said, leaning in and brushing my neck with his lips. "I do spend a lot of time fantasizing about Serina. The things I want to teach her to do with her mouth."

I purred and wrapped my arms around his waist, sliding my hands up his back, underneath his shirt. I kissed him and then pulled back to undo his buttons. He stood still, watching me, before reaching out again to touch my breast.

"I'm certainly going to miss these," he said.

He reached for the hem of my shirt and I raised my arms as he pulled it over my head. I always felt a small thrill when it passed over my head, blinding me, leaving me completely vulnerable. It was incredibly erotic. He tossed my shirt to the ground, gathered me up in his arms and kissed me.

After a moment, I broke away.

"I have an idea," I said.

I walked to the closet, wearing nothing but my bra and jeans, and grabbed one of his ties from the rack. I walked back towards him and held it up.

"Blindfold?"

He smiled.

"You or me?" I asked.

"Oh, definitely you," he said.

I could see him growing hard.

"But you're the one leaving," I said.

"Therefore, my choice."

He took the tie from my hand and moved behind me. He wrapped it around my eyes and tied it tightly behind my head. The world went black. I felt his hands drop to my back as he undid the clasp on my bra. Then he ran his hands back around front, taking hold of my breasts. I leaned back against him.

"You like that?" he asked.

"That, my love, never gets old."

He chuckled and squeezed my nipples lightly, causing a heavy moan to escape my lips. One hand traveled down over my belly and he single-handedly worked the button and fly, then used both hands to ease my jeans down my legs. He made sure to wrap his hands completely around my legs, causing an incredible sensation of warmth to pass through my body as he moved down.

He left my underwear on and took my hand to lead me to the bed. I climbed on and lay down. I was so incredibly turned on. My breath was coming quick and shallow. I couldn't keep still and I started to whimper as I waited, not knowing when he would next touch me.

And then I felt it, his finger trailing down my jawline, light as a feather. Wait. It was a feather. He'd taken one of the ticklers we'd bought in Amsterdam and was using it to trace a line down my jaw, to my neck, and down to my navel. I arched my back, begging him to continue. He stopped and started moving upwards again. This time he paused to pay special attention to my breasts, lightly passing the feather over each one and then making slow, lazy circles. I was moaning uncontrollably by this point, which only served to encourage Matt to keep going.

"God, I'm going to miss those sounds," he murmured.

He trailed the feather back down towards my navel, then mercifully continued on, playfully passing it back and forth between my legs. Even I had never heard the noises I was making before. He was positively delighted.

"Feel this," he said.

He took my hand and guided it towards his cock, which was rock hard. I closed my hand around him, slowly stroking him.

"Turning you on turns me on," he said, his voice thick. "I honestly think I could come just watching you get off."

"Oh, god..."

He passed his hand lightly between my legs.

"Allie, your panties are soaked."

"I want you so badly."

"I can see that. And feel it."

He slid my panties aside and I felt him slip two...no, three fingers inside, using his thumb to gently rub my clitoris. Within seconds I was screaming his name, bucking wildly on the bed as the orgasm overtook me. It was so sudden, so violent—like a magic wand orgasm, but better because it involved Matt. I could feel every nerve ending in my body. I was electric. I could smell the fabric softener off the sheets and Matt's cologne. I could hear the slow drip of the tap down the hall. It was like I was hypersensitive to everything due to my lack of sight.

"Shit," he muttered.

When I could catch my breath, I ripped off the blindfold and looked at him, dumbfounded.

"You're disappointed?" I asked.

"I am. I had such plans."

"Oh," I said, sitting up and getting onto all fours. "We're not done yet."

I crawled toward him and wrapped my mouth around him, and he let me for a moment. He ran his hand through my hair as I teased him, then took him in deep. He moaned, tightening his grip on my hair, and then gently moved my head away.

"Stay like that," he said.

He climbed into position behind me and guided himself in. I braced my palms against the mattress and he began to move inside me, holding my hips. I closed my eyes and succumbed to his rhythm, pushing back to meet his thrusts. I dropped down on the bed, my chest flat against the mattress with my ass still up in the air. He was in so deep.

"Matt," I said, breathless. "I think I can…"

He reached one hand around and slid it

between my legs, using his thumb to rub my clitoris, pressing it against his cock as it drove in and out of me. I moaned as he increased his speed, feeling my orgasm build.

"I'm going to come, Allie, I can't—"

I reached down with my own hand to help him, knowing just the thought of both our hands touching me at once would be enough to get me there. Within seconds, we were both coming, moving in unison as he wrapped his arm around my stomach, pulling me up against him. We both fell to the bed, tangled up in each other, breathing heavily, and he was running his hands up and down my body. I just reached behind me and held onto his thigh, squeezing, letting him know I loved him.

"I love you, too," Matt said.

We spoke the same language.

# CHAPTER TEN

I heard the distant sound of the alarm and rolled over in bed, instinctively reaching for Matt. Like every other morning that week, I had awoken forgetting he was gone. The good news was that one week had already passed, and in three more, he'd be home. I had precious little time to get the house in order, and with that thought in mind, I leapt out of bed and pulled on a pair of sweats.

I grabbed my phone on the way to the bathroom and checked my texts. I smiled, as sure enough, my morning wake up message from Matt was there. *Love you, beautiful.* There was also a text from Lynn, informing me she'd be stopping by that afternoon.

After getting dressed, I was enjoying a cup of tea in the living room when the doorbell rang. It was still early, so I knew it couldn't be Lynn. I went to the door and found Lily, a flushed smile on her face and a tray of brownies in hand. I opened the door wide to let her in and Loki ran happy circles around her, causing her to stumble. I reached out to save the brownies.

"You're in a good mood this morning," I said, smiling.

Ever since I'd told Lily to go home and masturbate, she'd been a changed woman. Much less high-strung, much more talkative. The poor woman had been sexually repressed her entire life and was just discovering what her body could do. I was almost jealous.

"It's a beautiful morning," she said.

"It's twenty below zero."

"Whatever."

Lily peeled off her jacket and made her way into the living room, curling up on the couch. I followed behind, amused.

"Let me ask you," I said. "Have you let Chris in on the fun yet?"

She looked at me, shocked.

"You mean, tell him?"

"I mean, show him?"

She flushed a deep red.

"No. He wouldn't understand."

"I'm not so sure about that," I said. "I've yet to meet a man who wasn't interested in sex."

"Well, you've met Chris."

Subject closed. She leaned forward, picked up a magazine off the table, and started flipping through. I took a seat on the chair and reached for my tea.

"Would you like something to drink?" I asked.

"No, that's okay."

I got up and walked into the kitchen to retrieve the brownies, a knife, and a couple of plates. I brought everything back into the living room and proceeded to cut up the brownies, offering a plate to Lily. She looked at it a moment.

"Oh, what the hell. Sure."

I handed her the plate and she took a delicate bite of out of the brownie. She made a surprised sound of pleasure and I looked at her and laughed.

"You made them. Did you expect them to suck?" I asked.

"No, I've just never had these."

I reached for my brownie and took a bite. It was delicious. I downed it in two bites and cut off another small square. It quickly followed its predecessor.

"So what brings you here this morning, Lily? Not that I'm not always happy to see you."

"I just wanted to bring these over. As a thank you. For changing my life. I know you smoke pot and all, and I thought these might be fun."

I had been in the middle of cutting a third brownie and stopped with the knife mid-air.

"These are pot brownies?"

"Oh! Yes! I thought I mentioned that."

"No. You certainly did not. Lily. I ate two."

She shrugged, confused.

"Is that a lot?"

"Well, my plans for the day are shot."

"I'm so sorry," she cried.

I just laughed.

"It's okay. It's just the last thing I expected from you. I can't believe you ate one."

She shrugged.

"Seems I'm all about trying new things lately."

We spent the rest of the morning giggling, and I did end up helping myself to that third brownie. I made us some Thai peanut noodles for lunch, something Lily had never even tasted before. We were laughing about something when the front door opened and we heard Lynn call out.

"Al? You here?"

"In here, Lynn!" I shouted a little too loudly.

Lynn wandered into the living room with an amused look on her face.

"What's going on?" she asked.

"Well, Lily here brought me some delicious brownies she baked. After I downed two, she mentioned they were pot brownies, so we're basically just fucking around. Wanna join us?"

Lynn rolled her eyes at us and continued toward the stack of boxes in the corner, grabbing the box cutter off the table on her way. My phone buzzed and I checked to see who it was. Matt. It was 9:00 p.m. his time. He must've just gotten in for the night. I answered the phone and waved off the girls as I got up from the couch and left the room.

"Hey," Matt said.

"Hey, yourself."

"Miss me?"

"So incredibly much."

"Are you masturbating?" he asked.

"Every day. And I wear your underwear when I do."

I heard his breath catch.

"Instant boner?" I asked.

"Yeah. Something like that. Fuck, Allie, I miss you so much. Come."

"I'm not coming, Matt. You'll be home in three weeks. Work hard and make it faster. I want to get the house done. Then we can go wherever you want."

"Promise?"

"I promise. Trust me, by March I'll be sick of being pent up in this place and be dying for a break. Take me somewhere nice."

"Done," he said.

"I love you, Matt Goldberg."

"I love you, Allie Styles."

I put my phone back into my pocket and went back into the living room, where to my absolute shock, Lynn was slicing off a piece of brownie for herself. I looked at her, eyebrows raised.

"Whatever," she said. "I'm seeing Dave after. I've discovered sex is fun when you're high."

*

When Lynn and Lily left at around five, I grabbed Loki's leash and took her for a walk. We enjoyed a nice brisk stroll around the neighbourhood. She was still getting acquainted, which meant we were stopping at every tree. It was close to six by the time we got home and as we were about to turn into the courtyard, I saw Louisa opening her front door.

Seizing the opportunity, I stopped and

waved at her, hoping to catch her attention.

"Hey!" I said. "Louisa, right?"

She turned and looked at me. She looked to be about 40, with curly brown hair that hung a little past her shoulders. She was wearing a suit under her winter coat, with dark tights stretching into black winter boots. She didn't look scary, or crazy, or bitter. She looked tired. She offered me a small smile.

"Hi. You're Allie, right?"

"Yes. It's nice to meet you."

Louisa smiled, then looked around awkwardly.

"Would you like to come in for a minute? I can put on some coffee."

I was shocked. Not what I expected.

"Sure, just give me a sec and I'll bring Loki home."

"That's okay," she said. "Bring her. I like dogs."

Another surprise.

I walked up the front steps and followed Louisa inside. It was like stepping into another time zone. All the curtains were shut and it was dark and cluttered. The furniture was from the previous century, all brocade and florals. The walls were covered in black and white photographs, with a few in colour scattered here and there. It felt claustrophobic. I was aching to rip back the curtains and open the windows.

Louisa watched me take it all in while reaching for my jacket and Loki's leash. I handed them over.

"I know," she said. "The place belonged to my mom. I inherited it from her when she died and I haven't gotten around to redecorating yet."

"Oh. I'm so sorry. Was it recent?"

"About five years ago."

"Ah," I said, not sure where to take conversation from there.

I followed her into the kitchen and she turned to me, embarrassed.

"I don't actually have any coffee," she said. "I'm a tea drinker."

"Me, too," I laughed. "It's perfect."

And then we proceeded to spend a very pleasant half-hour in which we talked about the neighbourhood, our neighbours, and our work. She was in family law. I, of course, was a restaurant critic. She was a perfectly lovely woman, and I couldn't understand what Rob and Lily had been going on about. At one point, I decided to investigate.

"So are you friendly with any of the other courtyard residents?" I asked point-blank.

"I pretty much keep to myself," she said.

"You invited me in."

"I liked your dog."

I just laughed. We finished our tea, I thanked her for the visit and returned home.

*

As the days passed without Matt, I used the time to really get to know our neighbours. At first, it was just a distraction. Matt and I had never been apart this long since we got together, and I missed him terribly. But eventually, I found I was enjoying myself and my independence and getting to know some good people. Jason was amazing and rapidly becoming a close friend. Lily was Lily, and I fell for her the moment she told me she had her first orgasm. She felt like a bird under my wing. I was even growing fond of Sophia, as well as incredibly curious about the whole open marriage situation with Mark. I'd yet to spend any time with Hailey, but I was looking forward to it. Living next door to a fireman? *Hello.*

In truth, they were all great. Even Louisa. We spent a few more evenings together, and I invited her for dinner one night. She had a very stressful job, and I felt she was happy to finally have someone to unload on. Over dinner, she told me her old friend from high school was coming to visit.

"That sounds lovely," I said.

"Well, his dad just died and he has to take care of the estate."

"Oh," I said. "I guess not so lovely. But at least you get to see him. When was the last time?"

Louisa looked up at the ceiling and let out a low whistle.

"Fifteen years, maybe?"

"What happened?"

"Nothing happened," she said. "Ian and I just grew apart. He was an artist. A sculptor. I was going to be an attorney. Our paths just went in separate directions. And when I got married—"

"You were married?" I asked. That was new information.

"Yes. I was married for almost ten years. Divorced a year before I moved into this house."

I was silent, waiting to see if she'd go on. I certainly wasn't going to push it.

"We met in college. Love at first sight kind of thing. I fell hard. Then we went to law school together and got married. He was a corporate lawyer, I was pursuing a career in civil rights."

"Civil rights? I thought you said you

practiced family law."

"I do. I'm a divorce attorney."

I started, then laughed.

"Divorce attorney. Funny that falls under family law. Should be anti-family law. How'd you end up there?"

"I went through a nasty divorce. After that, I decided no woman would go what I went through."

"Ah," I said and fell quiet once again. It proved to be an excellent technique to get her talking.

"I came home one day and found him screwing his secretary on our couch. Our fucking couch. But he was a shark, and despite the fact that he had cheated on me, he still managed to take me for everything I had."

"Holy shit."

"Yeah."

"Well," I said. "At least now you're protecting other women. That's got to feel good."

"Except all I see every day are families being torn apart. It's really depressing."

I nodded. I could definitely see that. Matt and I were both fortunate to come from loving, stable families but I had plenty of friends who weren't so lucky.

"Anyway," I said, changing the subject. "Tell

me more about Ian. Where does he live now?"

"I have no idea. Last I knew he was traveling around. But that was years ago. I guess I'll get the scoop tomorrow when he arrives."

"Was there ever anything between the two of you?" I asked.

Louisa laughed so hard I thought she'd start crying.

"No. Ian was... Well, he was that guy everyone loved. I was quiet and shy. We only knew each other because I was assigned as his peer tutor in high school. Somehow we became friends and stayed friends for many years. We were very close, but I was never in his league. Never even entertained the idea."

I looked at her, waiting. She laughed.

"Allie. Ian was a player. He could have any woman he wanted. He did not want the little brainy kid who tutored him in history and English. Besides, I met my ex so soon after we started college, it was never really an issue."

I picked up my fork and played with the crumbs on my plate leftover from dessert.

"Well, whatever. I'm curious to hear how it goes tomorrow. Come by once he's gone."

Louisa smiled, and I realized I'd made a friend.

# CHAPTER ELEVEN

"Hey, Sunshine."

I smiled, eyes still closed from a long night's sleep. I opened them and saw Matt standing over me, his face about six inches from my own.

"What are you doing here?" I asked, still groggy.

"I wanted to surprise you for your birthday."

"It's my birthday," I murmured, finally waking up.

"It is."

"Ha. I forgot."

He leaned in and kissed me, gently at first, then with increasing need. I reached up and locked my arms around his neck, bringing him even closer to me. His hand immediately went to my breasts, working their way inside my tank top. I moaned and arched my back, having missed his touch for over three weeks.

He lay down on the bed next to me and leaned in to take my nipple in his mouth. His hand worked its way south and slid into my panties. He stroked me, causing me to squirm and cry out.

"So wet," he murmured.

"Please, Matt…"

He continued with his slow, lazy strokes. Fireworks were going off in my head and everything was swimming before me. I closed my eyes.

"Please, what?" he asked.

"Please make me come," I begged.

He slid two fingers inside and pressed up against my g-spot while his thumb found my clit, applying pressure from the outside, too.

"Oh, god—"

He licked his way up my neck, taking my earlobe between his teeth.

"What else do you want me to do?" he whispered in my ear.

"I want you to fuck me."

"Mmm… How do you want me to fuck you?"

"Hard. I want you to fuck me so hard."

As soon as the words were out of my mouth I exploded, coming with an intensity that only follows three weeks of separation. I cried out his name and opened my eyes. To my shock, I was alone. I looked around the bed as the mid-morning sunlight came in through the window and realized I was absolutely alone.

And then I realized I wasn't. I turned to look toward the door, and there stood Matt. Flesh-and-blood Matt. He was holding his suitcase in one hand and his chin was pretty much on the floor. He swallowed and dropped the bag.

"What did I just witness?" he asked.

"I think I came in my sleep."

"You think?"

"I was sleeping."

"You didn't even touch yourself."

Matt was breathing so heavily I could hear him from across the room, which he then crossed in two strides. He pulled back the sheets and ripped off my panties. Climbing up on the bed between my legs, he placed his hands on my inner thighs, spreading them as far as they would go. And then he dove in.

It was like I was water and he hadn't had a drink in months. Matt had gone down on me *many* times since we'd gotten together, but it had never been like this. I fell back on the bed and raised my hips in the air, riding his face as he devoured me. I grabbed his hair, clenching my fists and bucking my hips, screaming his name. He just went in deeper.

"Oh, god, Matt. I'm going to come. Matt—"

He shifted his attention to my clit, swiping it with his tongue before taking it in his mouth. I cried out, and he growled. I felt the vibrations throughout my body. It drove me insane and I raised my hips again, pressing myself into him. He moaned, taking my clit between his teeth. As his mouth closed around me, my body erupted with a volcano-like intensity. Matt slowed down, still caressing me with his tongue until he felt the last of orgasm pass through me.

He worked his way up towards my face and kissed me. He meant it to be a quick hello, but I wrapped my arms around him and kissed him back, deeper. I ran my fingers across his shoulders, loving the feel of him beneath me once again. He pulled away and looked at me.

"I missed you so much," he said.

"Let's fuck," I said.

He laughed, then looked a little embarrassed.

"I came," he said.

"What? When?"

"When you came."

I popped up in bed.

"Are you fucking with me?"

I looked down at his pants. He was not fucking with me. I looked back up at him.

"Allie, watching you in your sleep like that? That was the hottest thing I've ever seen in my life. And we've seen some things. And then, just the taste of you…When you came in my mouth I just…"

Just listening to him was turning me on, and I felt the heat course through my veins. I had just come twice in quick succession, yet there was that familiar throbbing once again. I leaned down and kissed his chest, tracing a line with my tongue towards his nipple. I took it between my teeth and gave him a gentle nip. He put his finger under my chin and tilted my head up toward him.

"Did you miss me?"

I moved up and answered him with a kiss. A long, slow, deep kiss that tasted of coffee and me. For once I didn't mind the taste of coffee. I pressed my body up against his and brushed my lips against his ear.

"Make me come again."

*

Several hours later, we were sitting up in bed, tangled up in the sheets and smoking a joint. I was resting against him, finally sated.

"So," I said, finally able to speak. "What are you doing home?"

"I wanted to be home for your birthday."

I gave him a smirk.

"You could've told me," I said.

"Nah, would've ruined the surprise. Besides, I might've missed the show. And trust me, I'll be jerking off to that memory for many years to come."

I passed him the joint and wrapped myself around him.

"I never want to be apart that long again," I said.

"Agreed."

He ran his hand through my hair and I looked out the window. It must have been noon by then, but neither of us bothered to look at the clock. As soon as he came home, the outside world ceased to exist. I knew that for at least the next 24 hours, it was just me and him. We had already agreed not to even answer the door. Wasn't the usual way I celebrated my birthday, but it was just perfect. I didn't want a cake or candles or presents. I just wanted Matt.

"So what have you been up to here?" he asked.

"Making friends," I said.

"Why am I not surprised?"

"We lucked out. Such a great bunch of

people. I know you got to meet most of them at the impromptu wedding reception, but I've really gotten to know a few of them and all I can say is, well done on the house, Matthew."

I kissed him on the top of the head, in the same spot he always kissed me. He laughed and gathered me up in his arms.

"Are you grounded now?" I asked.

"For a while, at least. There's nothing in the works that I've heard of."

"Good. Where are you taking me?"

He laughed and gave me a squeeze.

"Let's go away at the end of March after all the families are done with spring break. Although I did notice that you finished up the house. Well done, Alison." He kissed the top of my head.

I sighed and sunk further into him. I never wanted to move. While I'd managed to keep myself busy with writing and the house, I had always felt his absence. Like a piece of me was missing. Just being there with him, safe in his arms, the heat of his body warming mine—that's all I needed. And of course that delicious Matt scent. I reached up and traced the scar over his eye. He closed his eyes, an expression of sheer pleasure settling over his face. That I caused that look meant everything to me.

I ran my finger up his leg, starting at the

knee and ending at his inner thigh, just below his crotch. I watched as he stirred to life, smiling to myself that I could raise him at my will. I raised my eyes and caught him staring at me, lips slightly parted.

"Again?" he asked.

"Again."

I leaned over and took him in my mouth. I repositioned myself on all fours and stuck my ass up in the air. He was rock solid in no time at all, reaching underneath me to stroke me while I sucked his cock. The first spank caught me by surprise, causing me to yelp—a sound I think he very much enjoyed judging by the way he strained in my mouth. But then I braced myself, using one arm to support my weight while I wrapped the other around his shaft, starting slow, steady, firm strokes as I licked the head.

When the second spank came it sent shivers of ecstasy through my body. Matt had a way of making me feel dirty in the sexiest possible way. The second spank was quickly followed by numbers three and four, until Matt finally said, gruffly, "Climb on."

I swirled my tongue around him one last time and then straddled him, sliding down onto him, feeling him fill me as I began to move against him. He reached up and grabbed both my breasts, squeezing as I increased my speed, riding him faster and harder. I covered his hands with mine, leaning into him until I felt my clitoris rubbing against him, the friction building until I grabbed his wrists and cried out, coming for the umpteenth time that morning. He bucked up against me, hips snapping as I felt his orgasm shoot through his body. I collapsed on top of him, buried my face in his chest, and lay still, trying to catch my breath.

"That was amazing," I said after a few minutes of silence.

No response. I lifted my head and looked up. He was fast asleep.

# CHAPTER TWELVE

The next morning, Matt and I were having a hasty breakfast together before he left for the office. He was reading something on his phone, his brow furrowed.

"What's wrong?" I asked.

He looked up at me, distracted. He shook his head a little, then put his phone in his pocket.

"Have you heard of the Corona virus?"

"The one from Wuhan? Yeah. What about it?"

"I was just reading that there was a confirmed case in Israel this past week. While I was still there."

I straightened up and looked at him, concerned.

"You worried?" I asked.

"Nah."

"It's already taken over Italy. They're all in quarantine."

"I know. But one case, Al, and I wasn't even anywhere near where the patient was."

He leaned in and gave me a quick kiss. I got up and walked him to the door. As I watched him walk down the long pathway to the street, I saw an incredibly handsome man who looked to be in his early forties walking up Louisa's front steps. *That's Ian?*

I walked back into the house and shut the door, wanting very much to call Lou and see what was going on, but opted to wait and let her come to me. I ended up watching as he came and went over the next several days until curiosity got the better of me and I picked up the phone.

"Hello?"

"Lou? It's me, Allie."

"Allie! I keep meaning to stop by," Louisa said.

"Well, from what I've seen, it looks like you've been busy."

"You mean Ian? He just needed a place to crash for a few nights, so he's staying with me. It's been great catching up."

"Catching up or exploring new territory?"

"ALLIE!"

"Just wondering," I said.

"Well, wonder no more. Purely platonic over here. Sorry to dispel any fantasies you were having."

I smiled to myself, said goodbye, and put away my phone.

I was very curious to see where that went.

*

A couple of weeks later, Matt came home while I was going through travel sites at the dining room table. We'd decided to go for one of those last-minute deals since we didn't care where we ended up. He came over to kiss me hello and the look on his face was grim.

"You don't think we're going anywhere, do you?" I asked, assessing his expression.

"I don't. Look what's happening in other countries. And now we're talking about 'social distancing?' I don't know, Allie. I wouldn't get my hopes up."

Matt was right.

Over the month of March, we watched in amazement as the city slowly shut down, bringing life to a complete halt. Matt was still hard at work, just doing it from home. As much as the pandemic freaked the shit out of me, I was elated to have him around all the time. He took the guest room as his office and we met for lunch every day. Sometimes in the evening, we'd bundle up and have a drink on our porch, just for the opportunity to socialize with our courtyard neighbours from a distance. Porch-time quickly became a thing.

Often, late at night I'd sit outside and smoke a joint. I'd look around the courtyard, wondering how they were all passing their time. How Sophia and Mark were getting along all alone. If Rob was dying without his direct lines of gossip. If Zach and Casey had hooked up—those two were so hard to read. I could've imagined how Lily and Chris were getting along, but I was dead curious about Louisa and Ian. I never got that one-on-one time with her, and I was dying to know. He was *hot*. I had a hard time believing he was living under her roof and she wasn't getting laid.

As I came inside from one of these evenings, I found Matt waiting for me in the downstairs hall, by the foot of the stairs.

"What's up?" I asked.

"Bedtime," he said.

He had that gleam in his eye, and I knew sleep was the furthest thing from his mind. I'd just put out a new column that morning, so I had an inkling of what had stirred him up. I'd written about Serina. I walked over to him and put my hand on his chest.

"Why don't you go find us a bottle of wine and some glasses, and I'll meet you up there," I said.

*

I slid the wig out of my drawer and fit it on my head, grabbing the box of bobby pins while trying to keep it in place. I had picked out a white lace bra and panties—Matt was still into innocent Serina—and checked my reflection before climbing into bed.

Matt walked through the door a few minutes later. He looked at me and the corner of his lip curled up, his eyes filling with lust. He groaned somewhere deep in his throat.

"Serina," he said. "As much as I've missed you, and am delighted to see you, I actually have a date with my wife tonight."

I tilted my head to the side, looking up at him. He walked over and sat down on the bed next to me. He reached and, one by one, unclipped each pin and gently removed the wig. He smoothed my hair down and leaned in to kiss me. Then he looked down, eyeing my lingerie appreciatively.

"That can stay," he said.

I reached up and stroked his face, searching his face for a clue of what was going on behind those sea-green eyes.

"What's going on?" I asked.

"Not a damn thing. I want to make love to my wife. I've been watching you all day, moving around the house, drinking your tea, brushing your hair out of your face."

He reached over and hooked his finger under my bra strap, sliding it down and leaning over to kiss my bare shoulder.

"I just want to touch you. Kiss you. Feel you against me."

He continued his trail of kisses up to my neck, brushing his lips against my ear.

"Be inside you," he whispered.

I moaned.

He slipped the other strap off my other shoulder and repeated his entire routine on the left side. I was swooning by this time, trying desperately not to come undone. He put his hands on my face and pulled me close, kissing me until I saw stars. Then he brought his lips back up to my ear.

"I don't need wigs. Or fancy underwear."

He reached behind me and unhooked my bra with a practiced move. He cupped my breast, running his thumb over my nipple.

"It's just you. *You* turn me on."

"Oh, god, Matt—"

"Shh…"

He leaned forward and took my nipple in his mouth, running one hand down between my legs and into my panties. I groaned, writhing on the bed.

"Do you want me?" he asked.

"Yes."

"Do you love me?"

"Oh, god, yes."

"Do you want to have my baby?"

"Oh, god, oh… what?"

I pulled back and looked at him. He gave me a sheepish look.

"Are you serious?" I asked.

"Dead serious."

"You want a pandemic baby?"

"I want an Allie-and-Matt baby."

I'd be lying if the thought hadn't crossed my mind. I was 33 years old, and while I didn't want to waste time, I also hadn't wanted to bring it up so soon after the wedding. But as usual, Matt and I were on the same page. And as usual, he was the one with the balls to bring it up. I reached down and undid his pants, sliding my hand inside, finding him hard and ready.

"Show me what you can do."

# Beginnings

Other books by Sydney Campbell:

**Allie Styles Romance Series**:
*Temptation (Book 1)*
*Deception (Book 2)*
*Reckonings (Book 3)*
*Beginnings (Book 4)*

**Courtyard Tales of Contemporary Romance**
*Reawakening*
*Redemption*
*Reckless*